E. Smith

Roller Skating Made Easy

E. Smith

Roller Skating Made Easy

ISBN/EAN: 9783337389826

Printed in Europe, USA, Canada, Australia, Japan

Cover: Foto ©Andreas Hilbeck / pixelio.de

More available books at **www.hansebooks.com**

ROLLER SKATING,

Its origin and history, theory and methods of practice,

names and descriptions of movements to be learned in

Plain and Fancy Skating, Figure and Combination

Skating, also Records of Fast Skating, and Rules,

ROLLER SKATING

MADE EASY.

THIS IS THE SOLE

INSTRUCTION BOOK

FOR ROLLER SKATING,

AND IS INDISPENSABLE TO ALL SKATERS.

A Healthful Exercise and most Graceful Accomplishment
Quickly and Easily Learned,

PORTLAND, MAINE.
PUBLISHED BY E. SMITH, (P. O. Box 1898).
1884.

PREFACE.

WE present this unpretentious little volume to the public with the hope that it may enable those who carefully study it to learn the principles of skating, and a correct system and method for practicing the same.

Without some such knowledge it is only by much hard work that one can become an expert skater; the fact that many skaters, able to perform difficult movements with considerable expertness, are not graceful in their motions and appearance upon skates, is due to a lack of proper instruction in systematic methods.

Every one knows that to become a good musician it is necessary to learn the system upon which it is founded, and the correct methods by which it should be performed. No one can attain great proficiency without acquiring this knowledge; the one who by aid of natural talent alone, without due study of system and methods, becomes a performer, never goes beyond mediocrity.

Let skaters, whether they are novices or already somewhat proficient, bear this fact in mind, and by the study and practice of proper methods they can effect the satisfactory improvement sure to result therefrom.

If our words serve to make easier the paths whereby grace and perfection in skating may be reached, and stimulate to practice the skaters who have ceased to try for further improvement, as also those among beginners who fear to attempt more than merely rolling around the rink, then the mission of the Instruction Book will be accomplished.

The book is intended to be an aid to teachers at the rinks, by being the means of preparing pupils to fully comprehend what the teacher may show them in practice, as well as to practice by themselves without demanding of the teacher constant repetitions.

The "Instructions to Beginners," if carefully studied, will give the novice a thorough knowledge of proper methods for acquiring the preliminary steps.

In the chapter upon "Fancy Skating," the "rolls" are first described, and the skater should become proficient in all these before attempting more difficult movements.

It is impossible to give within the limits of this little book descriptions of all the tricks and feats performed upon skates, but we may safely assert that after a skater has acquired ease and grace in the performance of all the movements herein described, there need be no hesitation in attempting any movements known to skaters.

The diagrams will assist the reader in understanding the instructions and the curves to be described; the positions of the feet however, in some instances and notably in the illustration of the cross-roll, are not shown as exactly as might be desirable for the instruction of novices; yet they are sufficiently correct for practical purposes we trust, if viewed in connection with the descriptions, which instruct the reader in regard to the relative positions and angle of the feet at the moment each step is taken.

There are persons, who, from prejudice or lack of knowledge of the practical value of a book of instruction, are inclined to doubt the benefits to be derived therefrom. To all such we will merely say, compare the performances of skaters who have learned systematically, practicing step by step in accordance with well defined methods, with the skating performed by those who have learned by hard practice and main force alone, without proper instruction or attention to the rules for acquiring grace.

By means of instruction in the proper system and method of skating, one is enabled to make rapid advancement, to avoid acquiring an awkward style, and to attain a degree of skill such as cannot otherwise be reached.

All skating, whether of plain movements or the most difficult figures, is governed by certain scientific principles and rules, which must be learned and practiced if one wishes to become an accomplished and graceful skater.

In the following pages we endeavor merely to give such instructions as will convey to the reader some knowledge of the fundamental principles and methods of skating, and serve as a convenient reference during practice. We submit the book with the following indorsement of one who is well and favorably known to the public.

Mr. Robert J. Aginton, who is the peer of any skater in America in grace and perfection of execution of his movements upon roller skates, attributes his skill to the careful study and practice of a scientific system, and upon reading our proof sheets, says that he has "practiced by just such methods as are taught by the Instruction Book."

THE AUTHOR.

ORIGIN AND HISTORY OF SKATING.

THE derivation of the modern English word skate shows its meaning to be shoot or slide. Italian *scatta*, a slide. Dutch, *Schaats*. In old English the word was spelled " scate."

Skating, as a means of locomotion and a pastime, has been in practice many centuries. The exact origin of skating is unknown, but it undoubtedly originated in a northern clime, where the natural bodies of water are ice-bound during a large portion of each year.

The history of Roller Skating is more brief and less obscure than that of skating on ice, to which the more modern pastime no doubt owes its birth.

Skating upon ice probably owes its origin to the necessities of the people of northern climes in traveling long distances over frozen surfaces. One naturally turns to the history of northern races for information on this subject, but the allusions therein to skates or skating are meager. Southern nations are presumed to have had no knowledge of skates and their use, and there appears to be no term in the Greek or Roman languages that refers to this subject.

The Scandinavians have been famous as skaters for centuries. Formerly long strips of wood turned up at the forward end were used for skating over ice and snow. Such skates as these were used by the Finns in traveling over snow and ice, and their use gave the people the name " skrid finnai "—sliding Finns. The modern Norwegian snow-shoe is of a somewhat similar form, greatly exaggerated in size, and being designed for sliding over hard snow is quite unsuitable for use on soft snow after the manner in which American snow-shoes are used.

Wood and bone appear to have been the materials of which skates were first made. Such skates have been found in Holland, Sweden, Iceland, and elsewhere. Bone skates were used in England in the twelfth century, and an author of that period describes skaters as "binding under their feet the shin bones of some animal, and taking in their hands poles shod with iron which at times they strike against the ice, they are carried along with as great rapidity as a bird flying."

In the old Runic poetry a hero says, in a poem called his "Complaint": "I know how to perform eight exercises: I fight with courage; I keep a firm seat on horseback; I am skilled in swimming; *I glide along the ice on skates;* I excel in darting the lance; I am dexterous at the oar; and yet a Russian maid disdains me."

Referring again to the Runic poetry, we find that skating is there written of as among the highest accomplishments of the people of the North. The hero just quoted says, "I glide along the ice on skates," in recounting his athletic accomplishments. Another hero of the same poetry boasts that he could "traverse the snow on skates of wood."

In the "Edda" occurs the following: "When the king asked what the young man could do who accompanied Thor, Thialfe answered, that in running upon skates he would dispute the prize with any of the countries. The king owned that the talent he spoke of was a very fine one."

In the same, written about 800 years ago, the god Uller is represented as distinguished by his beauty, his arrow and skates.

Modern Roller Skating is undoubtedly an outgrowth of the ancient skating on ice, and neither is likely to become obsolete.

The ice skate was probably first designed solely for utility in every day life, unlike the modern roller skate, which was devised for the purposes of amusement and healthful recreation.

The invention and general introduction to public use of the roller skates, has made skating popular in localities where ice skating is utterly impracticable at any season of the year; and also, on account of its many advantages, roller skating is fast becoming popular where ice skating may be enjoyed with certainty a portion of each year.

Out door skating upon ice will never be entirely superseded, for aside from its frequent availability in northern regions as an amusement and a useful means of locomotion, it has its peculiar charm.

Roller skating, however, has decided advantages in very many respects as a recreation. It is independent of clime, season, or the inconstancies of weather. The skating surface is good at all times. No ice to be too soft, or too hard, or too rough. Roller skating can be more easily learned by novices, and may be indulged in without exposure such as might be detrimental to delicate constitutions; facts which are of especial benefit to ladies and children. No danger of drowning nor of wet feet, attends this exercise, which is less violent than skating upon ice, requires less strength of ankles, and therefore is more to be enjoyed by ladies accustomed to city life. It is not only healthful and invigorating without being exhausting, but its practice teaches one to acquire a well-balanced and graceful carriage. In fact it is a graceful and healthful recreation such as should be promoted and perpetuated.

By the published accounts of this subject it appears

that the first inventor of the Roller Skate on record was Joseph Merlin, born in 1735, in the town of Hay, Belgium.

In 1819 a patent was granted in France to one Petitbled for a device involving the principle of the modern roller skate. These skates were "straight runners," no provision having been made for change of direction without raising the feet. Later, an Englishman named Tyers invented a skate with five single wheels in a row, arranged so that only two of them had a bearing on the floor at the same time.

In 1828, another skate named the "Cingar" was patented in France, and this skate was used in the rendering of a scene in Meyerbeer's opera "Le Prophete."

Twenty years later another skate was in public use, and since then the numbers of patents sought and granted for roller skates have been very great.

Probably the greatest single improvement ever made in the modern roller skate was that of Mr. James L. Plimpton, an American, who, by the device of a vertical axis with an oscillating movement, produced a skate such as enabled the wearer to guide himself at will in curves similar to those performed with skates on ice. Patents on the Plimpton skate were obtained in January, 1863, in the United States of America, and in England August 25, 1865. The Plimpton patents have now expired, and there are innovations constantly being made toward improvement.

Within the last few years the public interest in roller skating has been rapidly increasing throughout the United States; so that there are now rinks of a permanent character erected in nearly every state and some of the territories, from Maine to California, and from Dakota to Texas.

The health and pleasure to be derived from the

exercise of roller skating, deservedly render it a most popular recreation in summer and winter, for both sexes and all ages. The large permanent rinks of the better sort now established in New England and elsewhere throughout the United States, are gradually attracting the attention and patronage of fashionable and cultivated society.

The *Boston Herald* of Dec. 30, 1883, states, in regard to one of the five roller skating rinks in that city, the significant fact that "the number of elegant equipages that have been seen at the entrance indicates the character of the patronage."

Roller Skates, and the modern roller skating rinks, afford to the weak as well as to the strong the means of enjoying the graceful and invigorating exercise of skating, whereas ice-skating has generally been regarded as an amusement suited only to persons in robust health, accustomed to outdoor sports. The robust and accomplished ice-skater finds that the execution of difficult movements is no more fatiguing with the rollers than upon the ice, and a speed as great can be attained upon the rollers, while equal grace may be displayed.

To all beginners Roller Skating has the advantage of being more easily learned, and therefore becomes an amusement more available to the majority of persons, old and young.

To business men and others of sedentary habits, skating is a most excellent means for preserving health and good spirits, by affording an invigorating but not exhausting exercise and agreeable diversion.

Let ladies whose weak lungs or ankles and general lack of vigor forbid long walks or violent outdoor exercise, learn to skate on rollers, and thenceforth indulge habitually in the gentle graceful exercise of roller skating. They will be pleased to find as a result that a very appreciable benefit may be derived therefrom, as well as pleasure.

Physicians who have turned their attention to the modern pastime of roller skating, and acquired accurate knowledge thereof by practical experience, have very generally recommended it as one of the most beneficial exercises of the age, healthful and invigorating to the old and young of both sexes. Of course excessive indulgence, as of everything else, may be injurious.

We have not devoted space in this connection to descriptions of the various forms and merits of American Roller Skates and the improvements that have been made, because we have examined and tested but few of them; but attention will be given to this subject in a future edition, if the manufacturers enable us to do so.

In writing of modern skating, it is interesting now to recall the record of Mr. William H. Fuller, a young American, who left New York in 1865, and gave exhibitions of roller skating while crossing the continent to California. From San Francisco he sailed to Australia, practicing on shipboard during the voyage. After remaining many months in Australia he went to India, Turkey, Egypt, and then to Russia, in the frozen North, where one might naturally expect to find skating in its greatest perfection ; and even there he "astonished the natives" by his skill in "figure skating," such as seemed marvelous to the Russians.

It would be difficult and perhaps invidious to name any one skater of the present time as pre-eminent. Their numbers are rapidly increasing, and we hope to give in a future edition of this book some mention of the most noted skaters, in connection with descriptions of the special performances in which each excels. The best performers are constantly learning something, as well as the beginners, and although comparatively few will attain the utmost perfection of skill, everyone may learn the way thereto by the aid of the INSTRUCTION BOOK.

INSTRUCTIONS TO BEGINNERS.

"Observe that merely rolling round the rink
Is not so much like skating as you'd think."

For the better understanding of the instructions that follow, attention should be given to the terms used in describing the position of the feet during the various steps and movements.

Gliding Foot. The sustaining foot, or that one which bears the weight of the skater in gliding.

Balancing Foot. The raised foot, that serves as an aid in preserving the equilibrium or balance of the body.

Leading Foot. The advance foot. Whether the motion be forward or backward, this is the foot advanced in the direction of motion, thus leading the other foot.

Following Foot. The foot not in advance, but following after the other. In backward skating this foot would be the one farthest in front of the skater as then facing.

In ordinary skating the "gliding foot" is the leading foot at the beginning of a step or glide, and the "balancing foot" is the following foot at the start.

The Outer-edge. This term implies the outer rollers of the skates, and an outer-edge glide is one performed with a pressure brought to bear wholly or chiefly upon the outer rollers. This is effected by a side turn of the foot, but not of the skates, and the inner rollers are not raised from the surface.

The Inner-edge. This term implies the inner rollers of the skate, and an inner-edge glide is performed with the pressure on the inner rollers. If the foot is turned but slightly, the curve described by the glide will be an arc of a large circle. If turned more, the curve will be sharper.

The Surface. The word "surface" is used to designate the floor or surface upon which the skating is performed.

Many who have already learned to skate fairly well, as well as novices, are recommended to read the following

SUGGESTIONS.

Do not try to start too fast or abruptly.

Do not be afraid of falling, nor struggle too violently when a fall is imminent or unavoidable. It is better to expect to fall occasionally, and learn to go down easily. You will acquire more confidence in skating, when you know by experience that you can fall repeatedly without danger. When you find yourself obliged to fall, bend the knees suddenly, and thus drop down instead of tipping over at full length. You will be much less likely to receive a hurt thus.

Have confidence. You should bid farewell to timidity after making the circuit of the rink once alone, but do not be too bold until you can do this much.

Do not look at your feet while skating. Of course it is necessary for a learner sometimes to look at the feet while taking new steps, but it is well to avoid doing this too frequently. Acquire the habit of carrying the head and body erect, with the eyes directed toward objects upon their level.

The head should always be held well back, but not stiffly.

The body, when in forward motion, leans slightly forward, but should not be in a stooping posture. Expand the chest, and keep the shoulders thrown back as far as possible. Don't bend forward, but incline the whole figure.

The legs are always bent at the knee when taking a step. The leading one but slightly and just as the step is taken, and immediately thereafter the knee should be straightened. The balance is more easily and gracefully maintained upon the gliding foot with the leg straight, beside thus bringing the least possible strain upon the muscles. The balancing foot, however, is always carried with bent knee, more or less according to the figure being executed.

The arms should hang naturally and loosely at the side as in walking, with elbows and fingers slightly bent, and the palms of the hands toward the body.

Do not swing the arms violently about, nor hold them stiffly in one position.

Do not acquire awkward habits of clutching with the fingers, holding the arms out stiffly from the body, etc. All such tendencies may be readily overcome, as the beginner gains in confidence and proficiency, if due attention is given to the subject.

Don't try to learn too much at once. Learn to understand and acquire the preliminary steps first. The most rapid advancement in skating, as in other exercises, may be made by thoroughly learning the rudiments as a substantial foundation for what will follow. Study well the suggestions and instructions to beginners, restraining over-eagerness, and practicing one movement until able to execute it equally well with either foot before trying another; and when precision and perfection have been accomplished in all the movements to be found in that part of the Instruction Book devoted to " Instructions to Beginners," you will be able to astonish yourself and others by the rapidity, ease, and grace with which the evolutions of Fancy Skating may be acquired.

Study the Instruction Book, and practice the steps

at home.   When at the rink do not practice too long at a time.   Rest frequently, and refer to the description of the movement you wish to practice.

GRACE.

The form of a Venus or Adonis is not essential to grace. Absolute perfection in the human form is rare indeed, but those less favored by nature may, by proper attention to correct positions, acquire a grace approaching that which is natural to well-proportioned forms.

An erect position, with shoulders and head well back is most conducive to grace, and to best attain an erect position in skating, the sustaining knee should be straight, and the feet near each other.

A movement to be graceful should be made without apparent effort. Skating, which requires so little effort, is the peer in grace of any exercise or motion for the human form, and is not surpassed in this respect by dancing. This statement will not be questioned by any one who has witnessed the graceful evolutions and dancing performed upon skates by the best skaters of Canada and elsewhere.

The supple forms and light movements of ladies adapt them to excel in gracefulness, and awkward motions are more common to the sterner sex.

If careful attention is given to the suggestions and instructions of this volume, it should enable the reader to avoid awkwardness in skating, and to acquire a graceful carriage and movement, such as will bring ease and pleasure to the skater, and admiration to the beholder.

We will add to the foregoing suggestions an injunction of much importance.

Do not skate always in one direction.   This is equivalent to saying, don't become a one-sided skater, but learn to turn with equal ease either way, and glide in any direction with equal ease upon either foot.

Of course it is dangerous to skate in the opposite direction of a throng, and in all well regulated ice rinks the course of the skaters is reversed at short intervals.

This is effected by means of a signal, usually given by a single stroke upon the gong, and at intervals of about fifteen minutes, or between the intervals of music.

This is a custom we beg to urge managers of Roller Skating Rinks everywhere to adopt. It is a very serious drawback to skaters to be obliged always to skate around the rink in the same direction. It tends to make "one-sided" skaters, a fact well-known to experts who appreciate the necessity of being able to turn either way with equal facility. No one can excel in easy and graceful skating, without overcoming this one-sided tendency. This can only be done by practicing most frequently the turn which seems most difficult. Some persons naturally have less freedom of action in one direction, or upon one foot, than for the opposite. Such persons ought to practice the weaker or awkward side most.

The present custom at American Roller Skating Rinks of skating constantly around in one direction, is an immediate cause of "one-sidedness," and we hope to see it abolished very soon, and call on skaters everywhere to join us in urging this matter upon the immediate attention of Rink managers, to whom the advancement of skating is of direct interest.

THE DRESS.

For skating one should be dressed as for walking, and perhaps no especial directions upon this subject are necessary, except as regards the boots. The cus-

2

tom of putting what are known as "French heels" upon the boots of ladies and children calls for an especial warning. High, tapering boot-heels render it difficult for the wearers to carry the body in an erect and graceful manner, prevent them becoming accomplished skaters, and as the direct cause of many falls, *high heels are dangerous.*

Ladies ordinarily accustomed to wear boots with such heels should discard them for boots with broad, low heels, for the double purpose of utility and safety. This is a matter of much importance to ladies, whether beginners, or those who have already become somewhat proficient as skaters in spite of such a drawback.

It is safe to say that no person can become an expert, graceful skater, with extremely high or "cut-under" heels upon the boots. By a strict observance of these instructions in regard to boots, one will be well repaid by a rapid advancement in acquiring ease and grace upon skates, and in avoiding the most frequent cause of serious falls.

After one has attained proficiency in skating there is little risk of becoming too much heated by any indulgence in the exercise, but the beginner sometimes finds it otherwise; therefore ladies and children should take care to have the back and shoulders covered by some extra garment, while sitting down after skating, and should rest frequently, so as to avoid becoming overheated.

THE SKATES.

The skates should be of such size as will bring the center or axle of the front rollers exactly under the "ball" of the foot. It is customary at some rinks for skates of a larger size to be given out to beginners, but it is usually better to use skates of the proper size at the first, or else adopt them after a very few trials with longer skates.

To adjust a skate to the foot the heel of the boot should be placed as far back as possible, and the skate placed exactly under the center of the foot.

The skates are generally worn as " rights and lefts," with the buckles on the outer side. They should be firmly fastened to the feet, but not so tightly as to be painful, or to impede the circulation.

Clamp skates are generally worn with the linch-pins on the inner side, so as to avoid catching against the skates of another person when two are skating close together.

When new rollers are needed, they should be se-' lected of uniform width and vertical diameter for each set.

THE START.

Place the feet nearly at right angles to each other, and close together, with the hollow of one foot placed just behind the heel of the other. Bear this rule in mind always when rising, standing, starting and stopping. And when gliding the novice should not carry one foot parallel to the other at any time, as the balancing foot would not thus be in a proper position to guard or check the movement of the other, and the risk of a fall would be incurred with the feet parallel.

We will now suppose the beginner to be standing erect with the feet in proper position, at right angles to each other, ready for a start. Now raise one foot and place it directly on a line in front of the other, always toeing out with each foot. Put the raised foot gently upon the surface, and at the same instant incline the body slightly forward, in the direction the toe points, so as to bring its weight on that foot. This slight forward sway of the body and the simultaneous pressure of the weight upon the forward foot serve to propel the skater, who rolls along balanced on this foot until the other is placed upon the surface.

The feet should be kept quite close together, and when one foot is placed before the other the step should be a very short one,—in fact, just long enough to swing the raised foot in advance without striking its heel against the toe of the other.

No perceptible backward push should be made with the foot before raising it from the floor. The fault is often committed by beginners, especially by those previously accustomed to skate upon ice, of pushing forcibly with the gliding foot just before raising it, and in doing so allowing this foot to remain too far behind the other. Such skaters are also prone to keep their feet too far apart in skating on rollers, both sideways and by taking too long steps.

Preparatory to the glide let the novice imagine himself or herself, about to walk up a hill on a straight line, and required to place the heel of each foot upon that line at each step. In doing this one must take short steps, and at each step incline the body and bring its weight to bear firmly upon the ball of the advanced foot, as it is placed on the ground. In taking such a step the slight push or pressure of the supporting foot just as it is raised is not perceptible to an observer.

The Forward Glide. Plain forward progress on rollers is made by alternate zigzag lines, as in skating upon ice. It must be borne in mind before starting, that the toes are not to be pointed straight forward, thus placing the feet parallel to each other. *Toe out,* is a motto for the beginner to have constantly in mind during practice.

In comparing the steps taken in skating with those of walking, it may be said that in skating each step is taken as if about to cross the legs.

The toe is the last to leave the floor and the first to touch it, and whenever the foot is raised the toe should be pointed down. Thus the rear foot is raised, and with toe depressed and turned out is brought forward of the other foot, and placed upon the surface. At this instant the weight of the body is brought to bear upon the foot in advance by inclining or swaying the figure *in the exact direction in which the foot is pointed.*

The novice should at the outset, or as soon as able to maintain the balance upon one foot, learn to bear the weight slightly upon the outer side or "edge" of the foot. This will cause each glide to be made with a slight outward curve, such as is most in use for all plain skating. There is a tendency for novices to bear the weight somewhat upon the inner side or "edge" of the gliding foot, and such a tendency may be checked before becoming a habit, if the above instructions are borne in mind and practiced constantly.

Teachers at the rinks usually first instruct the novice how to walk on skates without attempting to glide along on the rollers, and continue the lessons until the proper method of placing the feet and balancing the body has been learned. The beginner, however, should not depend too much nor too long upon assistance or support, but with the aid of instruction first seek to become well-informed in regard to the theory and method of skating, and then practice alone as much as possible. It is by thus frequently practicing, that one acquires confidence and ease in balancing on one foot, with the other foot raised and held in proper position to place immediately upon the surface, to afford support when needed. Too much assistance from a teacher makes the pupil feel dependent upon his support, and less rapid progress in learning is made than by the beginner who depends upon an instructor only for occasional hints, corrections of faults, and as a guide rather than a support. A few minutes' practice with a teacher will prove of most value to those who study the Instruction Book beforehand, and use it for frequent reference afterward.

To prolong the glide it is only necessary to maintain the balance upon the gliding foot, and delay the advance of the balancing foot. By practicing in this manner one may soon learn to prolong the glide to eight or ten feet or more, and when this can be done with a feeling of confidence and security, other ordinary movements may be rapidly acquired, and skating with a partner enjoyed.

Always bear in mind that the chief motive power is the weight of the body brought to bear on the gliding foot, by turning, inclining, or swaying the body in the direction the foot points.

Do not try to propel yourself by violently kicking the surface behind, or thrusting back forcibly with the gliding foot when about to raise it.

The beginner should depend chiefly upon the weight of the body as inclined over the gliding foot, for the motive power.

The foot when raised should be brought forward slowly, with bent knee and toes pointing somewhat downward. This movement should not be quick and jerky, but gradual and easy, the last half of the movement being somewhat the quickest.

The placing of the balancing foot again upon the surface in advance of the other should not be done with a clattering thump or stamp, but as gently as possible, and at the same moment the weight is brought to press upon it by a gentle, graceful inclination of the body, scarcely perceptible to an observer when performed by a skillful skater.

Do not bend the knee too much, and thus acquire an awkward bobbing motion in skating.

Change of direction. Next after the plain forward glide the beginner needs to learn how to change the direction.

Stand upon one foot, and by turning this foot upon its side a very little so as to bring your weight to bear

upon the "outer edge," you will perceive that it will
cause the axle of the rollers to move in such a manner
as to make that foot toe outward. If gliding upon
the right foot this would cause you to turn to the
right, by the step or glide termed the "outer edge."
If gliding upon the left foot, the weight must be borne
upon its "inner edge," to effect a turn to the right,
and upon its "outer edge" to effect a turn to the left.

By alternately gliding upon the "outer edge" of
one foot and the "inner edge" of the other, one may
skate around an entire circle.

For the method of turning short corners the reader
is referred to the description of the "lap-foot" step.

When balanced upon one foot a change of direction
is greatly facilitated by whirling or turning the body
and shoulders around with each step, so as to immediately bring the skater facing in the direction the
gliding foot points.

THE FORWARD LAP-FOOT.

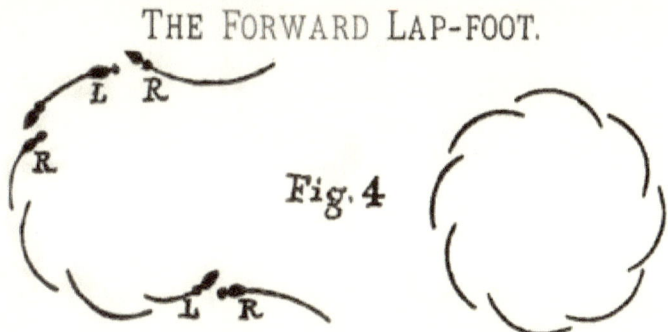

Fig. 4

Figure 4 illustrates the Forward Lap-foot step as
taken in turning to the left. In thus turning, the
weight must be borne alternately upon the "outer-
edge" of the left foot, and the inner-edge of the right
foot. If the turn to be made is an arc of a large
circle, a slight "lap" and a long glide may be made
at each step. For short turns a short glide and wide
lap is necessary.

The "Lap-foot" step is commonly used in turning short corners, or reversing the direction quickly without loss of speed. In fact if desired the speed may be considerably increased by this step, which is taken by crossing or lapping one foot over the other repeatedly.

When wishing to change your forward course to an opposite direction, by turning to the left, if gliding upon the left foot, bear your weight upon its outer edge, then bring the right foot well over in front, and as you place it upon the surface, bear the weight upon its "inner edge"; at the same instant raise the left foot and bring it quickly forward to succeed the glide upon the "inner edge" of the right foot by an "outer edge" step with the left foot. This in turn is succeeded by the "lap-foot" step with the right foot, gliding upon its "inner edge" each time.

To turn thus around a complete circle it is only necessary to continue repeating the steps described, which are alternately a plain outer-edge step with left foot, and a "lap-foot" inner-edge step with the right foot, for a turn to the left. For a turn to the right the outer-edge step with the right foot and a "lap-foot" inner-edge step with the left foot is taken.

THE BACKWARD LAP-FOOT.

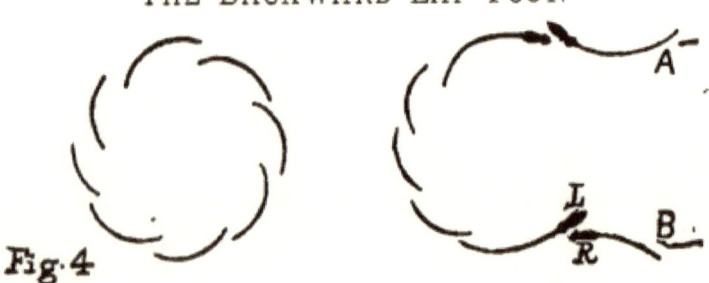

Fig. 4

This step is the exact reverse of the forward lap-foot step. The cut illustrates the turn as made by the skater approaching from the direction of "B."

At the termination of the outer-edge glide upon the left foot ("L"), the right foot is "lapped" over and placed on the surface, with the skater's weight borne upon its inner edge. These steps are repeated until the complete turn is accomplished, and the skater glides away in the direction of "A."

When making a turn by means of the lap-foot step, either forward or backward, the figure of the skater must be inclined sideways toward the center of the circle. This side inclination may be slight for a slow turn or a large circle, but for a sharp curve or high rate of speed the figure of the skater must be inclined so much that it would be impossible to preserve the balance if attempting to stand still in the same position.

THE STOP.

We will now assume that the beginner, having committed to memory the preceding instructions, has safely accomplished the start, the glide, and the turn, and now wishes to stop. To do this easily and at the exact place desired, will be rather difficult for an uninstructed novice who is apt to stop abruptly, by collision with some person or object not aimed at, or by catching hold of any person or thing convenient to check an uncontrollable career.

The most simple and easy method of checking and stopping the forward motion is placing the balancing foot at right angles in the rear, and close to the gliding foot, pressing it firmly upon the floor, while the body maintains its balance and weight upon the gliding foot. Thus the feet are in the exact position described for standing and starting, but the weight of the body is chiefly sustained by the foot in advance.

If necessary to turn from your course to stop at the desired place, it may be done with either foot in advance. For instance, in turning to the right the change of direction may be made by gliding either upon the outer edge of the right foot, or the inner edge of the left foot, with the balancing foot placed at right angles behind, with its hollow against the heel of the gliding foot.

The distance required in stopping may be regulated by graduating the pressure of the rear skate upon the surface.

The beginner should practice the "stop" very frequently, as after becoming proficient therein the skater will be enabled by this means to avoid collisions in a crowd, or in turning corners, or a stumble over some one who has fallen before, by suddenly and with unexpected notice checking or stopping his speed.

This is often necessary where the crowd is too dense to permit much change of direction whereby to evade such occurrences.

THE BACKWARD GLIDE.

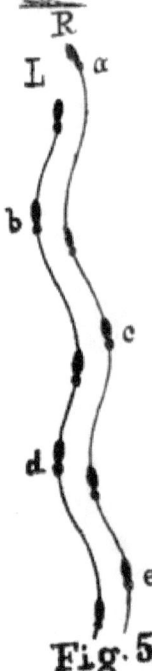

Fig. 5

The most easy method of acquiring a backward glide is by the movement termed "sculling" by skaters. This method is illustrated by "Figure 5," and it is the first backward movement to be learned by the novice.

Standing with the left foot at "L," and the right foot at "R," as shown in the illustration, the right foot is brought quickly around on its "inner-edge," with a forcible outward pressure upon the surface as it glides. As the right foot passes to the rear it is turned so as to bear the skater's weight upon its "outer-edge," and the left foot is then brought quickly around on its "inner-edge," in the same manner as was the right foot, with an outward push at the beginning of the curve. This push or outward pressure upon the surface is the means of propelling the skater, and is given with each foot alternately just as it is turned from the "outer edge," so that the push comes upon the beginning or first half of each "inner-edge" curve.

It is necessary to make this push or outward pressure somewhat forcibly at the start, but when a good speed has been acquired it can be maintained with slight exertion, and is not apparent to a beholder. When this method of skating has been practiced and learned so that it can be done with ease, one may begin to practice raising each foot immediately after the "inner edge" push above described, and prolonging the glide upon the "outer edge" of the sustaining foot.

A common fault with beginners in backward skating is to incline the body forward. The body should be as erect as possible. In backward skating, unless tripped by some obstacle, there is little danger of falling backward. The falls experienced by novices in backward skating are usually forward falls, and due to lack of confidence and the consequent forward inclination of the body. When gliding backward upon one foot the body should be erect, with the shoulders and head well back, the balancing foot carried in the rear of the gliding foot, and thus in position to be placed at once upon the floor to check any loss of balance.

The diagram (Fig. 5), shows the relative position of the feet, and it may be seen that each foot is alternately moved more quickly than the other. For example, at "b" the right foot is the leading foot, but before arriving at "c" it has been passed by the left foot, which has in the same time traversed a greater distance and now leads.

Then in turn the right foot is brought with a quick movement and outward pressure from "c," so as to become the rear or leading foot before arriving at "d."

The skater's weight is sustained upon each foot alternately, and the change is made at the instant that the foot brought around upon its inner-edge is turned to its outer-edge. The weight is borne on this foot at the same instant, which corresponds to the moment the balancing foot is placed on the surface in skating the backward roll.

Before entering upon the descriptions given in the chapter on Fancy Skating, we wish to urge beginners, and others who wish to skate with precision of movement, to count the time of each step or glide, *one—two*, etc., as in the practice of music. This will form the habit of using each foot alike, so that any step, roll, glide, or part of a figure executed on one foot, will occupy the same time as the same movement executed on the other foot.

FANCY SKATING.

A curved line is the line of beauty,
And motion in curves the skater's duty.
Let each movement represent a curve,
And do not from the proper method swerve.

FORWARD ROLL—OUTER-EDGE.

Fig. 1

The full-page illustration shows the correct attitude
in skating the outer-edge roll, and the diagram shows
the position of the feet in taking each step. The
former represents the skater at the beginning of a forward roll or glide upon the left foot; it might also
serve very well to illustrate the act of skating the
backward roll.

The "outer-edge" roll is the most graceful glide
performed upon skates, and as it is also easy to
acquire, it is the first movement we describe under
the caption of Fancy Skating.

"Figure 1" illustrates the glide and position of the
feet in taking each step of the plain forward roll.
"L" indicates the left foot, and "R" the right foot
on the diagram.

The beginner who has by practice thoroughly acquired plain skating as described in the preceding
"Instructions to Beginners," can acquire the Forward Roll in an hour. But further practice and at-

THE OUTER-EDGE ROLL.

tention to the following directions will be necessary
to acquire the desired ease and grace. This roll can
be gradually learned by lengthening the glide in
ordinary plain forward skating, bearing the whole
weight upon the " outer-edge " of the gliding foot and
inclining the body sideways at the same time. But
it may be learned with more precision and perfection
by practicing from a start and with constant attention
to the details of instruction.

Stand with the feet close together and nearly at
right angles to each other, the heel of the leading
foot placed against the hollow of the foot that is to
follow, with your weight borne upon the rear or " following " foot, by which you must propel yourself in
starting.

Now by a downward push of the rear foot and a
simultaneous inclination of the body in the direction
the other foot points, bring the weight to bear wholly
upon the outer-edge of the "leading" foot, as you
glide forward under the impetus thus gained. As this
push is given the "following " foot is instantly raised,
and placed in the same relative position behind the
gliding foot as at the start.

The glide should be prolonged so as to complete a
curve equal to a quarter circle.

It is during the last half of this curve that the
balancing foot should be brought forward, at the same
time turning the head and shoulders toward the point
where the curve will end, as if *carrying* the balancing
foot and leg around, and not swinging it independ-
ently of the motion of the body; always remember-
ing to keep the balancing foot pointed down, and
thus the toes lower than the heel.

The next step is taken by placing the balancing
foot forward upon the floor nearly at right angles to
the other, swaying the body sideways in the direction
it points, and at the same instant turn the following

foot so as to give a slight downward pressure on its
inner-edge, as the weight is brought to bear upon the
other foot, which now becomes the gliding foot. Remember that although the knee of the sustaining leg
is bent at the beginning of a glide, it should be immediately but not abruptly straightened.

In the execution of any "roll" the body should be
inclined "*sideways*," with the shoulder toward the
point that would be the center of a circle made by
the curve of the glide prolonged. Do not bend the
body forward, but keep it perfectly erect, and incline
the *whole figure* sideways, merely enough to counter-
act the centrifugal force. Continue the glide of the
second step for a quarter circle, and then repeat with
the other foot.

All the "rolls" should be practiced slowly and
with precision, with strict attention to every position
and motion of the feet and body, constantly guarding
against faults, until the correct method is so perfectly
acquired as to become a habit with the skater, who
henceforth becomes graceful in movements.

FORWARD CROSS-ROLL—OUTER-EDGE.

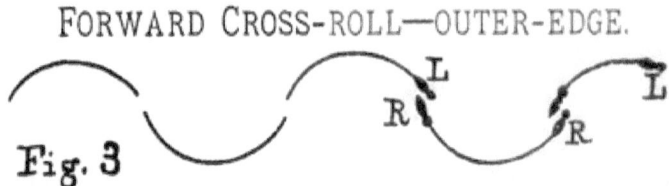

Fig. 3

Start in the manner described for the plain forward
outer-edge roll, and bring the balancing foot across in
front of the gliding, before placing it on the surface
again.

The diagram—"Fig. 3"—represents the first glide
as upon the left foot. The position of the feet is
shown for the beginning and end of each step or
glide, but this diagram does not show the exact angle
of the feet at the moment of taking a step. The

weight of the skater must be constantly borne upon
the outer-edge of the gliding foot, and as the change
is made from one foot to the other an impetus is
gained by swaying the body toward the direction
the gliding foot points. This impetus is increased
by turning the shoulders and body with a somewhat quick movement at the same instant, and the
push is given on the *outer-edge* of the gliding foot
as it is raised, therein differing from the push as given
for the plain roll.

Do not attempt to face toward the end of the rink,
but let your looks follow the direction the gliding
foot points; this direction is constantly changing, so
that you will alternately be brought to face toward
either side of the rink.

FORWARD ROLL—INNER-EDGE.

This "roll" is apt to be less practiced than the rolls
already described, because it is considered less graceful. Yet for one to become a good skater it is necessary to learn the inner-edge glides so as to execute
them with as much precision and ease as the outer-
edge movements, therefore practice of the inner-edge
roll should not be neglected.

Start as in plain forward skating, and bear the
weight constantly upon the inner edge of the gliding
foot.

The balancing foot should be carried in the rear in
the manner heretofore described, and brought forward
and placed on the surface at the end of each glide.

The impetus is gained chiefly by means of swaying
the body in the direction of each glide. Some skaters
carry the balancing foot in front, well toed out, and
held directly over the gliding foot, in executing the
inner-edge roll.

3

FORWARD CROSS-ROLL—INNER-EDGE.

This is the easiest and most graceful method of
skating the inner-edge roll, and differs from the preceding method described in the respect that the balancing foot is carried across in front of the gliding
foot to be placed on the surface. During the glide
the same relative position of the feet is maintained as
for the plain inner-edge roll. At the end of each
glide the next step is taken by toeing in the balancing
foot, as it is brought across in front of the other, and
in placing it on the surface the body is swayed in the
direction this foot points, and the weight brought to
bear upon its inner-edge. At the same instant a slight
push is given on the outer-edge of the rear foot as it
is raised. This movement is repeated at each succeeding step, and the glide should be prolonged to
describe a quarter circle. After this can be easily
performed, the skater should practice prolonging the
curve to an entire circle, and continuing it to a spiral,
thereby preparing himself for the more difficult figure
skating to be learned hereafter.

BACKWARD ROLL—OUTER-EDGE.

Fig. 2

This movement is easily learned after one has become proficient in the backward glide (Figure 5), by
prolonging the glide upon the outer edge and raising
each foot alternately as this is done.

Figure 2 represents the first glide as upon the right
foot (R). At the end of the glide the weight is
brought to bear upon the *inner* edge of the gliding
foot for a moment, and a slight push is given, as at

the same instant the other foot is placed on the surface, with the weight brought to bear on its outer edge. The push or pressure given on the short inner-edge curve at the end of each glide affords an impetus sufficient to carry the skater to the end of the succeeding glide.

As each foot is raised it should be carried to the rear of the other foot, in proper position to be placed upon the surface again.

BACKWARD CROSS-ROLL—OUTER-EDGE.

This movement is the reverse of the forward outer-edge cross-roll, and differs materially from the plain backward roll.

At the end of each glide the balancing foot is crossed over behind the gliding foot, and as it is placed on the surface, the skater should turn around so as to bring his whole person facing the direction the sustaining foot points. The push is given upon the *outer-edge* of the foot as it is raised at each step, and the turn of the body aids in giving an impetus to the succeeding glide. The body should be carried very erect, with the weight well upon the heels, and the figure inclined sideways toward the center of the circle of which the curve of each glide forms an arc. The curves thus described are precisely like those of the forward cross-roll illustrated by Fig. 3. In effecting the change from one foot to the other the push or pressure is given on the outer-edge of the gliding foot as it is raised, and not as in the plain backward roll by turning the foot to the inner-edge for the push.

The proper position of the balancing foot during each glide is immediately in the rear of, and nearly at right angles to, the gliding foot. There are various methods of bringing the foot around after raising it.

Some skaters prefer to bring the balancing foot to the rear quickly and at once upon raising it from the surface. Others bring the foot around slowly, quickening the movement a little on the latter half of the glide, and we deem this the better method.

The balancing foot may be carried close to the skating surface, or raised to any height or in any style suited to the taste of the skater. But whether the feet are moved quickly or slowly, and raised much or little, the skater should avoid abruptness, and seek to acquire ease and grace in all motions.

BACKWARD ROLL—INNER-EDGE.

This movement is an important one and somewhat difficult to acquire, and therefore it should be practiced assiduously until thoroughly learned. Too many are content merely with being able to skate backward by the inner-edge step, without regard to any method or grace in movement. In skating the backward inner-edge glide the skater should not face the direction the gliding foot points, but turn the body so as to face in the direction of the center of the circle of which the curve is an arc.

The start is usually made from a forward glide, and under the impetus thus gained, the skater turns and glides backward on the inner-edge, with the balancing foot held in the ordinary position behind the gliding foot, the sustaining leg straight, the figure slightly inclined in the direction toward which the glide is made, and the body faced as above described.

For example, when gliding on the right foot the body is faced to the left, and the skater in this position can glance over his left shoulder in the direction of movement, and avoid the collisions incurred by a front-face position. The body must be erect, and not bent forward at the hips.

Remember that while gliding on a curve the sustaining leg should be straight, as also the body, and the figure of the skater is inclined from the skate, and not bent at the hips. At the beginning and end of a glide it is necessary of course that the knee of the sustaining leg shall be bent.

At the end of each glide the next step is taken by placing the balancing foot upon the surface in the rear of, and nearly at right angles to, the other foot; the weight is brought to bear upon it, and an impetus gained by inclining the body back, at the same instant turning the sustaining foot and giving a push on its outer edge as it is raised.

The foot just raised is now carried to its position as balancing foot in the rear of the other, and in doing this the body is faced around so that the skater glides with the right shoulder leading.

The backward cross-roll is the reverse of the forward cross-roll, and after the movements of the above instructions have been thoroughly acquired by practice, the cross-roll may be easily performed.

THE SUBURBAN ROLL.

This is a graceful and favorite method of skating with a partner, and it affords good practice for the long inner-edge and outer-edge glides. Each curve is described by three glides, the first and last upon the outer-edge, and the middle glide upon the inner-edge, each succeeding curve being precisely similar. For example, if starting with the left foot outer-edge glide, continue the curve by a right foot inner-edge glide, this in turn succeeded by a left foot outer-edge glide; then begin the return curve by a right foot outer-edge glide, succeeded by a left foot inner-edge glide, and a right foot outer-edge glide to complete the curve.

Backward and Forward Turns.

Forward to backward turn on the toes.
Backward to forward turn on the heels.

These two general rules give the principle upon which all ordinary turns are made. There are various methods of turning upon both feet, and all of them are easily learned, as the skater advances in proficiency.

The turns from left to right and from right to left, should be practiced until each becomes equally easy of execution as the others. If at first it is more difficult to turn one way than another, practice the difficult turn the most.

A very easy way of turning from forward to backward is as follows:

Bring the balancing foot forward and place it on the surface so as to point straight ahead, and at the instant the weight is borne on this foot, turn the other foot on its toe without raising it (just as if about to assume the "spread eagle" position for a sideways glide), and bring it quickly back alongside its mate, as the body is whirled about so as to reverse the position of the skater, who is then in position to skate backward by any step that may be chosen.

The turn from backward to forward is most simply effected by making a short outer-edge curve, and turning on the heel of the gliding foot, the toe of the other foot resting lightly on the surface as the body is whirled about. The succeeding forward step is effected and an impetus gained by a push on the inner-edge of the gliding foot at the close of the turn, as the other foot begins the forward glide. In thus turning, both forward and backward, the balance of the skater is guarded and assisted by keeping the toe of the balancing foot upon the surface, until the complete turn is effected.

Proficient skaters usually employ both feet at the beginning of a turn only, or else turn upon one foot without any assistance from the other.

One foot turns are effected by whirling the body about, with the weight sustained at the instant of the turn according to the above rules printed in italics. It should be remembered, however, that although the turn from forward to backward is made with the weight sustained on the toes, this is only for the instant of the turn, and immediately the turn is accomplished the weight should be borne well upon the heel for the backward glide; and in turning from backward to forward the weight is maintained solely upon the heel of the gliding foot for the instant of the turn only.

THE PROMENADE.

The promenade step is a favorite method of skating in time to music, and when correctly executed it affords an easy and agreeable manner of changing the glide from one foot to the other. The ordinary promenade step is effected by placing the balancing foot across in the rear of the other, and bringing the weight to bear upon it, as at the same instant the other foot is brought around to the rear in position for a push which is given to gain an impetus. This movement may be executed without any precision or attention to the proper way of placing the feet, and in a jerky, awkward manner. But it may also be executed with precision of movement and in a graceful manner, if practiced according to the following instructions:

Do not raise the balancing foot from the surface while bringing it to the rear.

We will suppose the learner to be standing in proper position for the start, the feet at right angles to each other, with the hollow of the rear foot at the heel of the leading foot. The movements will then be as follows:

One—the first step is the push with the rear foot, and this gives the impetus for each glide.

Two—the second step consists in changing the glide to the rear foot by quickly placing it on the outer side of the leading foot, and bringing the weight to bear upon it. At this instant the feet assume the same position as for the change of glide in the cross-roll (see Figure 3).

For better understanding we will assume, for example, that the start is made with the left foot leading. The impetus is given with the right foot, immediately followed by step number "*two*," which changes the glide from the left to the right foot. The left foot is now brought around, well toed out and the heel raised, to the rear of and at right angles to the right foot; the steps, *one, two*, are now executed by the left foot in turn.

It is by repeating these movements alternately with each foot that each change of glide is effected.

There are various methods of performing the promenade step. The two movements may be executed in rapid succession at the change of glide, and each glide prolonged to a long roll. In skating thus, if the leading foot is quickly brought to the rear it must be carried there until the close of the glide, when it is again placed on the surface as before, and immediately made to assume the glide by step "*two*."

The usual method of executing the promenade, is by so managing the leading foot at the change of glide as to occupy the whole time of the glide in bringing it to the rear, in position for executing step number "*one*," and each succeeding step and glide may be thus performed without raising the entire skate from the surface at any time. Uniformity of movement is essential to grace in skating the various promenade steps, and the learner will be aided in acquiring this by adopting the method of counting time for each step.

Another method consists in giving the push when the balancing foot is just opposite, or at one side of, the gliding foot, instead of first bringing it to the rear as heretofore described.

A common fault in skating the "promenade" movement is committed by the skater not bringing the leading foot around to the rear in the proper manner, merely lifting it back, instead of turning the foot outward with the toe resting on the surface. The latter and proper method is much more graceful.

THE BACKWARD PROMENADE.

The usual method of skating the promenade backward consists in bringing the following foot around to the rear by a serpentine curve, similar to the corresponding movement in the "serpentine express," bending the knee of the sustaining leg slightly at each step, and crossing the foot in the rear as each succeeding glide is begun, with both feet kept continuously upon the surface.

THE SUBURBAN PROMENADE.

This graceful method of skating with a partner is similar to the "suburban roll," except that the "suburban promenade" consists of three glides upon one curve, and a change of direction for the return curve by means of the promenade step already described.

For example, start with an outer-edge glide, to be succeeded by an inner-edge glide upon the other foot, and this in turn succeeded by an outer-edge glide upon the first foot, all three glides being made in the

same direction upon one long curve. At the close of
the third glide place the balancing foot upon the surface in the rear, by the promenade step number "*two*,"
at the same instant bring the other foot around, and
by the promenade step number "*one*" give the impetus by which to prolong the first glide on the return
curve now started on.

The curves are similar to such as are described in
skating the long roll, but in the "suburban" roll each
curve is described by three glides, as has been previously mentioned, the middle one being an inner-edge
glide, and the other two are outer-edge glides or rolls.

The plain "suburban roll" is executed by making
the change of direction, as in skating the ordinary outer-edge roll, without introducing the promenade step.

THE SUBURBAN CUT-OFF.

This movement is similar to the three-step suburban
promenade, but with one of the three glides of each
curve omitted or cut off; so that each alternate curve
is performed by two glides, an outer-edge on one foot
and an inner-edge on the other. If the first curve is
begun by an outer-edge glide, it is completed by an
inner edge glide, the next returning curve is begun by
an inner-edge glide, and the next by an outer-edge
glide, alternately gliding upon each foot.

For example, start with an outer-edge glide on the
left foot, and continue the curve by an inner-edge
glide on the right foot. The next curve is begun
with an inner-edge glide on the left foot, and this
glide is succeeded in turn by an outer-edge right foot
glide in continuation of the same curve. We therefore come to the end of the second curve by an outer-
edge glide on the right foot, when the change to the
return curve is effected by the two steps of the regular promenade, the left foot being placed on the

surface in the rear, and the right foot quickly brought around to give the impetus for the outer-edge glide on the left foot that begins the third curve.

The sequence of glides would be, for first curve, outer-edge left foot, inner-edge right foot, turn ; for second or return curve, inner-edge left foot, outer-edge right foot, turn ; for third curve, outer-edge left foot, inner-edge right foot, and so on.

A curve may be started with either an inner-edge or outer-edge glide. If the second glide is on the inner-edge, the first glide of the next curve will be on the inner-edge of the other foot. If the second glide is on the outer edge, the first glide of the succeeding curve will be on the outer-edge of the other foot.

THE "STEP-OVER" PROMENADE.

This is executed by three movements. Start as in the plain promenade, and after changing the glide to the rear foot by movement number "two," step upon the toe of the leading foot, the toe of the boot resting on the surface. Then step over with the rear foot and begin the next glide upon it. For example, "*one*,"—glide on left foot ; "*two*,"—glide on right foot placed in rear ; "*three*,"—step on the toe of the left foot, which is still in advance, and immediately raise the right foot, bring it forward, and with a step over the other foot, place it on the surface, and upon it perform the first glide of the succeeding movement. The forward progress during the execution of the "step-over" promenade should be slow, and the successive movements executed in regular time.

THE "CUT-OFF" PROMENADE.

This graceful movement is performed by three steps, the first two corresponding to the plain promenade. For the third step the leading foot is brought around to the rear in the same manner, but instead of stopping at right angles to the other foot, it is toed back as in the "eagle" step and placed thus on the surface. A short backward glide is taken on this foot, ending with the inner-edge push which forms movement number "one" of the promenade step and gives the impetus for the succeeding forward glide.

For example, let the skater start with the right foot leading. The impetus is given by a push ("one") with the left foot, which immediately afterward beçomes the gliding foot by movement number "two." Now turn the body so as to face sideways from the direction of the glide, thus bringing the left shoulder ahead, as the right foot is turned around so as to toe back; now bring the weight to bear on the right foot, and terminate the short backward glide on this foot by an inner-edge push which gives an impetus for the succeeding outer-edge forward glide on the left foot. The movements are thus repeated, so that the third step of each is a backward glide, performed by each foot alternately.

In executing the "cut-off" promenade, the skater faces alternately in an opposite direction and glides forward in this position with the shoulder in advance. The first glide is made on the outer edge forward, the second is also a forward glide, the third a backward glide and the shortest one.

The motions of the skater should be uniform, graceful and easy, and not too quick. There are two methods of skating this movement; differing from each other only in the manner of executing the third or backward glide. This may be performed by placing the foot on the surface behind the other foot, or before it. The former is the easiest method for a slow movement and long glides; but the latter method— turning the foot before or on the inner side of the other* for the backward glide—seems to be most in vogue. The "cut-off" is also varied by prolonging the backward glide.

THE EAGLE.

The eagle, or "spread-eagle" as it is sometimes termed, is a glide performed with each foot toed out upon the same line. To execute this it is first necessary to acquire a momentum; one foot is then brought to the rear and turned so as to point back towards the starting point, the other foot pointing forward, and the skater thus glides sideways, or with one side in advance and facing at right angles to the direction of the glide. This movement may be performed with the feet far apart and the legs much bent at the knees, or the heels may be placed against each other. The latter method is the more difficult and can be easily acquired only by persons whose joints are flexible and adapted to such a position of the feet.

The *eagle inner-edge* consists of a glide performed with the feet in a similar position, with the weight of the body borne on the inner-edge of the skate, and a curve instead of a straight line is described by the glide thus made.

The *eagle outer-edge* is executed by bearing the weight upon the outer-edge, the body inclined somewhat backward, and gliding on the curve of a circle having its center behind the skater.

CHANGE OF EDGE.

It is quite important for the skater to become proficient in readily changing from the outer-edge to the inner-edge glide and *vice versa*, upon either foot, and in backward and forward movements.

Start as in the outer-edge roll and while gliding on

one foot change to an inner-edge roll, then to an outer-edge roll, and repeat with the other foot.

Practice this movement forwards and backwards until perfect ease is acquired, and you will be well repaid for the time thus spent by the facility with which many intricate movements may thereafter be readily performed.

THE SERPENTINES.

A serpentine is simply a continued glide upon the inner and outer-edge alternately, or a "change of edge" glide prolonged. This may be performed upon both feet, one directly in advance of the other, and forward or backward, or upon one foot.

The *eagle serpentine* is executed with the feet in the position described for the eagle movement, the toes pointing in opposite directions and the skater facing at right angles to the direction of the glide. By repeating the change of edge with each foot the serpentine movement is acquired and the glide prolonged by a uniform motion of the feet and body.

THE SERPENTINE EXPRESS.

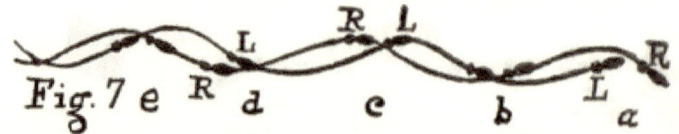

Fig. 7

Great speed can be attained by this movement, which is similar to the serpentine, but each foot alternately leads. The curves performed by either foot are the same in forward and backward skating, and are shown by the diagram (Fig. 7), which is intended to illustrate the backward movement.

The principle by which an impetus is gained is similar to that of "sculling," or the backward glide described under Fig. 5.

Referring to the illustration (Fig. 7), we will assume that the skater has already acquired a momentum and is at " a," with the left foot " L " leading, and " R," the right foot following. At " b " the skater's weight is chiefly borne on the left foot outer-edge, while the right foot is drawn back with a rapid movement, and a pressure on its inner-edge as it crosses the line of the other foot. By this rapid movement the right foot is brought to the rear, so that it leads at " c." The left foot now performs a curve across and back in front of the right foot while gliding from " c " to " d," where it is brought around with the quick turn and inner-edge pressure on the toe by which the impetus is gained.

In this movement both feet are constantly on the surface and the skating is performed by the feet and legs with the body held in one position, facing back toward the starting point, without turning from side to side. By employing the principle by which the impetus is gained in this movement the greatest possible speed in backward skating may be attained.

The relative position of the feet and the curves described in skating forward are similar to the same in executing the movement backward. In either direction the movements consist of the principle of " sculling " employed in connection with the method of crossing one foot alternately before and behind the other.

ENGLISH ROLL.

This movement is performed by placing the feet parallel and so close to each other that they touch, and by swaying the body alternately from side to side, accompanied alternately by a slight inner-edge and outer-edge pressure on the skates, an advance movement in serpentine curves is effected.

DECEPTION.

This movement is performed by taking steps as if walking in one direction while the actual progress is in the opposite direction. The steps may be taken either forward or backward, and the legs are crossed at each step.

In skating forward by the deception steps an impetus is first gained and as the forward glide is prolonged each foot is alternately placed upon its *inner-edge* behind the other; at the same moment glide the leading foot forward with a quick movement, and then immediately draw it back to the rear for the succeeding step on its inner-edge. At the moment the rear foot is placed on the surface the weight is brought to bear upon it, the advance foot is moved as above described with an outward turn of the toe, and the hips thrown forward by an almost imperceptible motion as the upper portion of the body is held well erect.

The forward deception movement is not easy to a beginner, because of the difficulty in placing the foot upon its inner-edge in the rear of the other. Practice the serpentine movement by starting with an inner-edge glide, and place one foot behind the other in taking each step. Remember that each step must be upon the inner-edge, and the glides short.

When the proper method of managing the feet and hips has been acquired the skater will be enabled to maintain a forward progress for an indefinite time, or until tired out.

The backward deception is the reverse of the forward movement and is performed by alternately placing each foot, well toed out, upon its *outer-edge* across in front of the other, and gliding back upon this foot; then the other is quickly brought to the front and placed on the surface, with the weight brought to bear upon its outer-edge, as in turn the skater glides upon this foot.

THE MUSIC STEP.

This consists simply of step number two of the promenade step, repeated once, twice, or more at the skater's option, in each glide. For example, when skating the music step in double time, as the weight is borne on the rear foot the leading foot is advanced and is then made to sustain the weight an instant while the rear foot is again brought up behind and alongside as before. This is done by two quick motions, to be succeeded by the glide. At each step the knees are bent and the steps and glides should be in time with the music.

THE GRAPEVINE.

Fig. 6

Last but not least among the fancy field movements we attempt to describe, comes the grapevine. In executing this movement the skater turns about so as to alternately face in opposite directions, forward and back, but does not make an entire revolution.

At the start the face may be toward the direction of the glide, but the first "whirl" brings the skater upon a backward glide and thus facing back toward the starting point. The next whirl brings the skater back to the position of the start, and facing in the same direction as then.

The black lines of the illustration indicate which foot leads during the progress of the glide, and the dotted lines indicate the following foot. By this

4

means the reader can perceive the exact point at
which one foot passes the other, as well as the curves
described by each foot. As in the "Serpentine Express," the feet describe curves precisely alike, and by
the method illustrated each foot is alternately in advance, with both feet constantly upon the surface.

Assuming that the start is made with the left foot
leading, the right is brought forward and across in
front of the left with a slight turn of the body to the
left; the curve is then reversed, the left foot following the right and passing it just as the skater arrives
at the point for the first "whirl," when he turns so as
to glide backward with the left foot leading. The
right foot is now brought by a serpentine movement,
across and back, in front of the left foot, the weight
being mainly sustained on the latter, and at the end
of this serpentine curve the second "whirl" is performed. This whirl brings the skater back to the position of the start, when the right foot is quickly
brought around as before, and the movement continued. Each turn is made upon the heel of one foot
and toe of the other, as illustrated by the diagram
(Fig. 6), and between the turns the legs are crossed.

Another method of skating the grapevine consists
of the same movements, except that at the first whirl
the right foot is immediately brought around to the
rear of the left instead of across and back in front.

The curves executed by each foot are precisely the
same as shown by the diagram, but instead of the left
foot leading on the backward glide after the first
whirl, the right foot is brought around to the rear and
made to lead, and at the next whirl brought forward
so as to lead on the forward glide as before.

By either method the impetus is gained by a pressure with the following foot at the turns; and the latter method, by which the foot leading on the forward
glide is made to lead on the backward glide also, is

the method most commonly adopted by skaters, and the start is made backwards.

The grapevine is not a difficult movement to learn after one has become proficient in the serpentines and turns, but not until such proficiency has been acquired will the skater be enabled to attain that uniformity of motion so necessary to an easy and graceful execution of this movement.

The double grapevine is performed in a similar manner, but instead of turning half around an entire revolution is made, and then an entire revolution back again. So that if the first turn is from left to right the next is from right to left, and the glides between the turns are all forward glides.

The grape-vine may also be performed on the toes. A similar movement varied in execution by the method of crossing the legs and turning the feet before each whirl is sometimes termed the "Philadelphia twist." This is a more rapid movement, but the curves described are similar to those of the grape-vine.

DANCING.

Dancing upon skates is such a pretty and graceful amusement that we hope to see it become as much in vogue and popular favor upon rollers as it deservedly is with skaters upon ice. When the learner has by practice and careful attention to the instructions heretofore given, become a good skater, and especially proficient in the turns and changes of edge, then waltzing may readily be enjoyed, as well as quadrilles.

For a quadrille the square should be formed of larger size than for ordinary dancing, as the movements of the skaters are more rapid in executing the figures. The greater distance between opposite couples enables the skaters to acquire an impetus for the turns, and a rapidity of movement in executing the figures in time to the music.

In waltzing the feet are usually not raised from the surface, but the steps and turns may be varied to suit the individual tastes of the skaters and the time of the music.

The beginner should practice alone until able to turn with ease in time to the music, before attempting to waltz with a partner, and constantly bear in mind that the dance is a succession of glides. The turns should not be made by means of a jump. Turn the toes well out in making the turns. The "cut-off promenade" and "grapevine" movements afford excellent practice for acquiring ease in waltzing. We would refer the novice to the remarks made in connection with combination threes and eights for useful hints in regard to dancing quadrilles.

TRICK AND FIGURE SKATING.

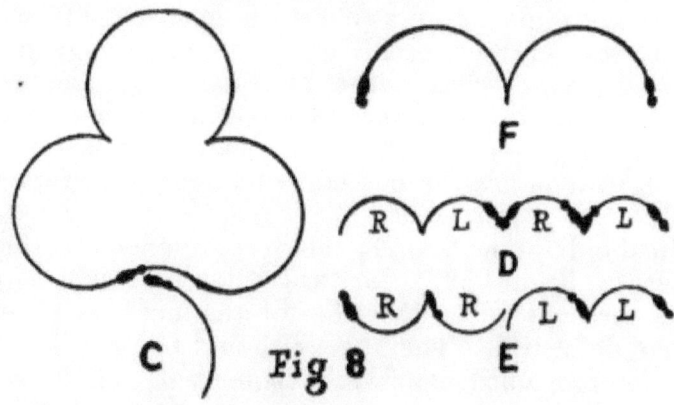

Fig 8

We begin this chapter with a description of the figure three. When the skater has practiced the various methods by which this figure can be performed, and has become thoroughly proficient in executing all of them well with either foot, the skill thus acquired will be sufficient for the performance of any figures or movements known to skaters, provided that equal proficiency has been attained in the movements heretofore described. We therefore commend to skaters the threes and their combinations as a most excellent practice, especially for acquiring more perfectly the turns, changes of edge, etc.

SINGLE THREE.

The curves described in this figure are illustrated by " F " in Fig. 8. There are four ways of executing the figure three, viz.: 1—first curve an outer-edge forward glide, turn on toe, second curve an inner-edge backward glide; 2—first curve an inner-edge forward glide, turn on toe, second curve an outer-edge backward glide; 3—first curve an outer-edge backward glide, turn on heel, second curve an inner-edge forward glide; 4—first curve an inner-edge backward glide, turn on heel, second curve an outer-edge forward glide.

In the diagram, Fig. 8, "F" represents the single three as begun by a forward glide and ended by a backward glide, as by either of the methods 1 and 2 above described. The threes should be practiced upon each foot until equal proficiency with either may be attained.

DOUBLE THREES.

"D," figure 8, illustrates the position of the feet when executing double threes by employing both feet, commencing at the right with a forward outer-edge glide on the left foot, the first curve thus described is succeeded by a similar curve described by an outer-edge backward glide on the right foot, and this in turn succeeded by an outer-edge forward glide on the left foot, and so on.

Omit the letters R and L and the illustration " D " will serve to show the same movement as performed upon one foot. A variation may be effected by describing three curves upon one foot before changing to the other foot.

Another method of performing double threes is to execute a complete three on one foot and then repeat on the other foot. For example, an outer-edge forward glide, turn,—inner-edge backward glide on same foot, turn; then an inner-edge forward glide upon the other foot, succeeded by an outer-edge backward glide on that foot.

FLYING THREES.

"E," Fig. 8, illustrates one of the several methods by which flying threes may be executed. In the illustration the first three is executed by a left foot forward outer-edge glide, and an inner-edge glide backward on the same foot. The next three is executed by an outer-edge forward glide on the right foot, succeeded by an inner-edge backward glide on the same foot.

There are several methods of performing the flying threes. Three curves instead of two may be described on one foot before executing the reverse curves upon the other foot.

Another method is to change from the last curve of the figures executed on one foot to the first reverse curve of the next without turning the body, employing each foot alternately.

THE CLOVER LEAF.

"C," Fig. 8, represents the clover leaf as executed upon the right foot. The clover leaf consists of the figure three curves prolonged so as to bring the skater around to the starting point in three glides or curves.

We will suppose the start to be made backward on the right foot, which describes a short serpentine and then executes an outer-edge backward roll, then turn and continue by a forward inner-edge roll, turn again and execute another outer-edge backward roll which is prolonged to the point of starting, when the figure is completed by an outer-edge backward roll on the left foot, the last glide forming the clover leaf stem as shown by the diagram. The figure may also be executed by starting with a forward roll.

The double clover leaf is performed by prolonging the finishing glide that forms the stem so as to make it a serpentine, and executing a second clover leaf at the end of this serpentine.

FIGURE EIGHT.

The figure eight consists of two circles joined together in such a manner as to resemble the numeral as usually printed. There are various methods of executing the figure eight, upon one foot, both feet, alternate feet, forwards and backwards, etc.

The eight may be performed upon one foot by first attaining sufficient impetus and then executing the first circle forwards, upon either inner or outer edge, and the second circle backwards.

In performing the eight by use of both feet an additional impetus is gained at the change, when one circle has been completed and the second is begun with the other foot.

LOOPS AND RINGLETS.

Loops and ringlets are executed on either edge of the skates and upon one foot, by starting with an impetus previously acquired and turning around constantly in one direction by gliding in short curves. The loops, as the term denotes, consist of more elongated curves than the nearly circular ringlets.

LOCOMOTIVES.

There are various methods of performing the locomotive movements, which are supposed to effect an imitation of the noise of a locomotive engine. They should be commenced slowly, and the steps gradually quickened until the greatest possible rapidity in succession of steps is executed, and the finish performed by gradually retarding the steps.

The same steps may be skated without noise by gliding the feet on the surface throughout the same movements. This method is certainly more graceful, while equally attractive to beholders, although the so-called "locomotive" imitation effected by the noise of placing the skates on the surface at each step is omitted.

SINGLE LOCOMOTIVE.

In this movement one foot constantly leads. If the left foot is the leading foot the start is made by placing this forcibly on the surface for a forward glide, then do likewise with the right foot by placing it on the surface in the rear, toed out, and glide forward on its inner-edge as the left foot is raised and immediately put down again in the same position. Then raise the right foot and toeing back place it on the surface, and perform a backward glide on its inner-edge as the left foot is again raised from and returned to the surface.

Thus it will be seen that the movement consists of the repetition of four steps, as follows: Leading foot forward, following foot inner-edge forward, leading foot forward, following foot inner-edge backward.

The steps with following foot are executed with this foot turned so as to be placed on the surface at an angle of about forty-five degrees to the direction of progress. The leading foot may be held so as to point straight forward, or it may describe a slight serpentine during the forward movement.

DOUBLE LOCOMOTIVE.

This movement is similar to the single locomotive and differs only in the change whereby each foot leads alternately. It is executed by bringing the rear foot in advance after the four steps have been taken, and making it the leading foot, while the same steps are repeated with the other foot, which then in turn is made to lead again.

Another method of imitating the noise of a locomotive engine consists in gliding forward alternately upon each foot, and using the balancing foot to effect the noise by tapping upon the surface as it is brought forward.

BACKWARD LOCOMOTIVE.

Glide backward upon one foot and with the other perform steps similar to those of the forward locomotive movement. If the left foot leads bear the weight upon that foot and draw it quickly back, at the same instant toe in the right and crossing it in front of the left place it on the surface. The right foot is then drawn back on its inner-edge, with a quick turn and a backward cross step on its outer-edge, executed in the rear of the left.

It will be seen that in performing the backward locomotive the diagonal steps are executed alternately before and behind the gliding foot, instead of each step behind as in the forward locomotive.

PICKET FENCE.

This movement resembles the locomotive, but the skater makes a sideways progress by means of zigzag steps, one foot constantly following the other. For example, if the skater starts with his left side in advance this position is maintained throughout the execution of the movement. The steps or glides are very short, and all of them are executed with the feet at an angle of forty-five degrees to the direction of progress.

Starting with a forward step or glide on the left foot, the second step is forward on the right foot placed across in the rear. The third step is backward on the left foot, and the right foot is crossed in front for the backward fourth step. Then the first forward step on the left foot is repeated, and so on. If the start is made with the skater's right side in advance, the right foot will lead constantly. A variation may be effected by alternating the leading foot.

SCISSORS.

This figure or movement consists of spreading the legs and drawing them together again, and it may be performed in a variety of ways. The plain forward scissors movement is executed by extending one foot directly in advance of the other as far as possible, the legs straight, the advance foot gliding on its heel and the following foot gliding upon its toe. Then the rear foot is brought forward so as to lead, and by thus alternating, the skater glides forward, and appears as if walking stiff-legged with long strides. The movement may be performed backward, but is more difficult to execute thus. Another movement, usually termed the "spread," consists of spreading the legs by toeing out, and allowing the feet to glide apart on the heels, with the legs straight, and then drawing the feet together.

The revolving scissors is a movement effected by a combination of the plain forward and backward scissors already described, and is executed by turning constantly in one direction as the rear foot is brought up, so that the skater faces forward and then backward alternately as the steps are executed; or an entire revolution may be made at each turn as another variation.

ONE-FOOT SERPENTINES.

In performing the serpentine movement upon one

foot the same principle of motion is employed as in the serpentine with both feet on the surface. The impetus is gained by the alternate pressure of the skater's weight upon the inner and outer edges of the skate, and a corresponding side sway of the body. The balancing foot may be carried in the usual position, at right angles in the rear, or swung to and fro across the path and in the rear of the gliding foot, or rested upon the gliding foot with the toe turned out, or in any way to suit the taste of the skater. The one-foot serpentine, forward and backward, affords excellent practice in acquiring a good balance and the change of edge upon one foot.

PIVOTS.

The term pivot is used to denote a curve or circle executed by a glide upon one foot while the other foot is held rested on the surface at the center of the circle. The principle employed is the same in all the various pivots. The figure of the skater must be inclined toward the center of the circle, as in executing the rolls and all of the longer curves, and the leg that describes the curve must be held as straight as possible.

The plain pivot is performed by gliding upon the inner-edge of one foot, either forward or backward, around a circle of about two feet radius. That is to say, the feet are about two feet apart while executing this figure.

As the body is inclined to one side in starting on the gliding foot the skater is enabled to locate the center of the circle and drop the toe of the pivot foot upon it, and it should be held there until the full circle has been described by the gliding foot:

To start a pivot, stand in the usual position of rest with the feet nearly at right angles to each other. Give an impetus with the rear foot and glide on the outer-edge of the leading foot, immediately placing the following foot close alongside in the rear and continue the curve on its inner-edge. Then at once raise the leading foot, and carrying it about two feet to one side, let its toe rest on the surface, in the center of the circle to be described. It will be observed that the start is effected by means of two steps corresponding to the "promenade" movement, except that the second step is taken on the inner-edge.

The outer-edge pivot, forward and backward, is performed by crossing the legs, one knee being placed against the leg under the other knee, and the feet crossed over as far apart as possible. The general instructions for the inner-edge pivot should be applied as far as is possible to the performance of the outer-edge pivot. The leg of the pivot foot should be crossed over behind the other leg.

While in the act of executing the pivot the position of the skater should be as follows: the body faced as the gliding foot points, the outer leg straight and controlled from the hip as it is brought around simultaneously with the turn of the body; the figure inclined to one side so that a straight line could be drawn from the shoulder through the leg to the gliding foot. The feet are at right angles to each other, the pivot foot resting on its toe.

The weight is sustained by both feet after the start, but wholly upon the gliding foot at the instant of starting. In the moment required for carrying the pivot foot to its position the glide is sufficient to enable the skater to assume the proper inclination of the body and fix the center point upon which the toe of the pivot foot must be placed. Remember that the pivot foot must be toed out, at right angles to the other foot, and if properly placed it should not move from the center point until the circle has been completed.

PIVOT EIGHT.

There are various methods of executing this figure, as the skater may employ the inner-edge, or the outer-edge rear cross pivot, or a combination of several pivots. A plain pivot-eight may be performed as follows:

The starting point should be at the center of the eight or where the two circles meet, and at that point the skater faces toward one side of the figure. Execute the first circle by an inner-edge pivot, and at its completion bring the feet close together, and the figure erect at the same moment, then execute the second circle by an inner-edge pivot upon the other foot. The whole figure should be executed with an even motion, devoid of any perceptible hitch or pause. After the skater has acquired skill in performing the eights but little impetus will be necessary at the start, as the motion is effected by means of properly controlling the inclination and turn of the body. With too much impetus it is difficult to hold the pivot foot in position so as to describe a perfect circle.

Each circle of the eight should be of the same size, and at the completion of the figure the skater is at the point of starting, and facing in the same direction as at the start. In changing from one circle to the other the balance of the skater should be preserved by avoiding any abrupt movement, as the relative positions of the feet are changed and the body brought into an erect position and inclined to the other side.

A combination pivot-eight may be performed as follows: Start on the first circle with a forward outer-edge pivot, the feet not too far apart, and when the circle is half described turn on the toes and complete the circle by a backward inner-edge glide. Continue on the second circle by a backward outer-edge glide, pivot-leg crossed behind, and when the circle is half described turn on the heel of the gliding foot and complete the circle by a forward inner-edge glide.

A similar combination pivot-eight may be performed by starting backward, and making three turns instead of two, one at each end of the figure eight and a turn in the middle, when the change is made from one circle to the other.

SPINS.

A spin consists of whirling upon one foot or both feet by repeated revolutions in one direction. The head and shoulders should be turned in the direction toward which the skater turns, the body held erect, and the arms may be extended each side, held close to the sides, or bent at the elbows so as to bring the hands up to the breast or shoulders.

The spins upon both feet are usually started by allowing the feet to glide apart, and then drawing them together forcibly.

A spin on one foot is usually started by gliding in a sharp curve upon either the inner or outer-edge; or by first performing a spiral under a strong impetus, ending with the short curve by which a spin is begun. The balancing foot is carried across in front of the sustaining leg, and is raised quite high by some skaters during the execution of the spin.

The number of revolutions possible in one spin depends upon the skill and endurance of the performer.

The wonderful rapidity and duration of a good spin are well illustrated by the performances of such well-known roller skaters as Mr. Robert J. Aginton, Mr. W. E. Livesey, and others. Mr. Aginton informs us that he has executed upward of three hundred turns in a single spin.

PIROUETTES.

A pirouette in skating, as in dancing, is a whirl or turn performed upon the toes. Or it may be likened to a toe spin, consisting of one turn, or two turns only. Pirouettes are introduced as variations in fancy and figure skating.

THE FIGURE Q.

The name of this figure is due to its resemblance to the letter Q in form as described by the curves executed. The figure is performed by starting with a one foot serpentine, at the end of which a "figure three" turn is made and a complete circle executed on the same foot. For example, start on the outer-edge forward and complete the serpentine on the inner-edge forward, then turn on the toe and execute a complete circle by a backward glide.

Or, start on the outer-edge backward and complete the serpentine on the inner-edge backward, then turn on the heel and execute a complete circle on the outer-edge forward.

There are eight ways of performing the Q, corresponding to the eight methods of starting. The start may be made on a serpentine and the circle described thereafter, or the circle may first be executed and the figure completed by the serpentine; and by each method there are four ways to begin, viz.: forward outer-edge glide, forward inner-edge, backward outer-edge, backward inner-edge.

This figure affords most excellent practice in acquiring a good balance, in change of edge and inclination of the body, and in the turns, and it cannot be too highly recommended to experts as a regular practice figure. The curves described can be varied, and need not correspond to the form of the letter Q.

JUMPING.

A facility in jumping upon skates is of much practical value in field ice-skating, but is less a necessity or accomplishment for roller skaters in a rink, although sometimes of advantage in Polo playing.   Various feats are performed by jumping, and among them is the " spread eagle " jump.   This is performed at full speed with the feet in the " eagle " position.   The eagle reverse is effected by jumping, and turning while in the air, so as to come down on the surface upon the same line and continue the eagle movement, with the foot in advance that was previously the following foot.

TOE STEPS.

Nearly all of the movements heretofore described, such as the grapevine, promenade, serpentines, threes, eights, waltzes, eagle, etc., may be performed upon the toes.   The skater should become proficient in balancing and plain gliding upon the toes before attempting difficult movements.   If this is not done the toe movements cannot be executed with that ease and grace which render them attractive.

5

Combination Skating.

The figures that may be skated in combination by two or more persons are almost innumerable. We will make no attempt to mention more than a very few of them, as the anticipated limits of our little volume have already been exceeded. Expert skaters are constantly devising new variations in combination skating, and there are many regular movements of which a full description would make a long chapter on the subject. We commend skaters to assiduously practice the threes and eights, so as to be able to enjoy dancing. To Rink managers we would say, introduce the quadrille as a never ending source of enjoyment for your patrons, not only for the skaters, who can become proficient in the necessary movements by aid of the *Instruction Book*, but also for their friends who will go to see the beautiful evolutions of graceful skaters.

Dancing.

In the list of combination figures dancing is easily first, for it affords opportunities for executing all the most graceful movements known to skaters.

Waltzes may be danced with the ease and grace that render a graceful movement the poetry of motion. We see expert skaters dancing the waltz alone upon rollers, but it is rare to observe any one waltzing with a partner in the roller skating rinks. And as yet the dancing of quadrilles in the roller rinks seems to be unknown, although both kinds of dancing form a

common amusement in the ice rinks we have visited.
We do not know of any exhibition in figure skating
more pleasing to spectators and to the performers,
than is afforded by quadrilles danced on skates by
proficient skaters This is especially true of double
quadrilles, each formed by eight couples.

As in ordinary European dancing, the figures of a
quadrille upon skates are not usually called out by
name. The dancers are supposed to be familiar with
the figures which are executed in regular rotation or
merely called by number by the leader of each set.
In America, however, where so many dancers allow
themselves to become dependent upon a caller or
"prompter," it might be necessary to post placards in
the rink giving a list of the regular figures of a quadrille in their proper order. And instead of the figures
being called at each change of measure in the music,
a large placard numeral corresponding to the figure
as numbered on the regular list may be displayed at
the band stand, so as to be readily seen from all
points.

If these few hints and suggestions result in the introduction of dancing as an additional rink attraction,
we shall feel that they have not been offered in vain.
We would refer the reader to the descriptions of the
combination figure eight as suggesting the methods of
dancing quadrilles on skates. .

REVOLVING THREES.

This movement is performed by two persons facing
each other, and joining hands, and in this position the
curves and turns of the "figure three" are executed,
each skater alternately gliding backward and then forward. The movement to be graceful should be rather
slowly performed.

Start with an outer-edge roll, one skater gliding

backward and the other forward upon the opposite
foot; at the end of the roll execute a turn, and by an
inner-edge glide upon the second curve of "figure
three," the skater who led at the start by a backward
outer-edge roll now follows by a forward inner-edge
roll; and the skater who faced forward at the start
now glides backward by the inner-edge roll.

The changes may be effected by turns upon both
feet or upon one foot, and the movement may be varied by turning at the ends of each alternate roll, by
reversing the turns, by separating and joining hands
again, etc. A similar movement in which the two
skaters perform the cross-roll, in connection with the
figure three turns, is termed the "Mercury."

COMBINATION EIGHTS.

The combinations of the movements known as threes
and eights may be elaborated into a great many variations, and these figures are employed in dancing
quadrilles. We will not attempt, however, to give a
description of the intricate (and yet to expert skaters
not difficult) movements that may be performed by
four or more persons, but merely devote a few lines to
a description of the plain eights. The start should always be made upon the right foot, and it is necessary
to remember this to avoid confusion when afterward
practicing the eights comprised in more intricate
movements. By this we mean that the first curve of
the figure itself should be described on the right foot,
and in the combination eights each skater should have
the right shoulder toward the center of the figure at
the start.

FIGURE EIGHT BY TWO PERSONS.

Three circles are described in executing this figure.
At the start the skaters face in opposite directions,

each facing toward one side of the figure eight to be described, the right shoulder of one skater opposite the right shoulder of the other, with the right hands clasped together. Now with a forward outer-edge cross-roll upon the right foot each skater describes a curve, then the hands are disengaged and each describes a circle by a forward outer-edge glide on the left foot. At the completion of this circle the skaters may clasp their right hands again and repeat the movement as many times as they choose.

The figure may be varied in execution by starting backward, and also by introducing the turns of the "threes" in the execution of each separate circle. The eight may be started from a rest, or by the skaters meeting while under an impetus, and each outer circle of the eight may be executed by the "pivot" step.

THE EIGHT BY FOUR PERSONS.

Five circles are described in executing this figure, the central circle forming one half of each of the four eights. The four skaters clasp right hands across each with the right side toward the center, and thus describe the first curve upon the right foot outer-edge; then disengaging hands each describes a circle on the left foot outer-edge.

The same variations that are adapted to combinations performed by two persons may be employed by four persons, starting forward or backward, employing either edge, the turns of the "three," etc.

THE EIGHT BY FOUR COUPLES.

This figure is executed precisely as the last described, except that the skaters move in couples. The positions at the start are the same, the four inner skaters cross right hands, the left hand of each being held by the partner, and thus the first curve is performed. The crossed right hands are then disengaged and each couple executes a circle on the left foot outer-edge.

The eight, as performed by two or four couples, is the principal figure employed in dancing quadrilles upon skates. Starting from a rest, with the four couples standing so as to form a square as in dancing the quadrille, the movements should be regulated so as to avoid confusion or any pause after these positions are left. The first two opposite couples should start slightly in advance, and the other couples reach their places at the center just after them, so that the first circle to be performed with clasped ·hands shall be commenced without a pause after the skaters start from the positions of rest. When in position at rest each couple is assumed to be on the outer side of the outer circle of the eight to be described by that couple, the inner circle of the eight being described in the center of the set. In leaving their positions the skaters should face somewhat to the right, and approach the center by an outer-edge glide on· the left foot, immediately changing to the outer-edge right foot glide, as the hands are clasped in the center.

COMBINATION TOE-STEPS.

The toe-steps may be executed in great variety by two persons, and some of these movements are very pretty, such as the "pivots," for example.

Some movements are attractive to skaters merely because they are difficult. There are but few movements executed entirely upon the toes that cannot be otherwise performed in a more graceful manner, and the same may be truly said of the movements performed entirely upon the heels.

There are many acrobatic feats performed upon skates that might be described in a chapter on combination skating, but space will not permit.

Fast Skating.

The speed possible to acquire upon roller skates appears to equal, or even exceed, what has been performed by the best skaters upon ice. At a championship match for fast skating upon ice in England, in 1867, the recorded time of the winner was 7 min., $4\frac{1}{2}$ sec., distance two miles, the course being one mile and return, the speed acquired being at the rate of one mile in 3 min., 32 sec. We do not mention this record as of the greatest speed possible to attain upon ice, but for sake of comparison with some of the best public records of roller skating at the present time. Possibly all previous records may yet be excelled.

All the roller skating is done in rinks where there are many turns to the mile, yet this fact does not seem to conduce to any reduction of speed; but on the contrary, the fastest roller skaters testify that the greatest momentum can be attained in making the turns, provided the rink is not too narrow. Except in starting the greatest speed is not to be attained by running upon the skates, as novices appear to think, and in long distance skating the strokes or glides should not be too short.

In fast skating the arms should not be swung to and fro, as this impedes the progress, neither should they be held too stiffly. The arms may be carried at the side, or with bent elbows so as to bring the hands to the breast.

In making the turns to effect a change of direction the weight should be borne mainly upon the inner foot, and for as short a time as possible at each step on the outer foot, as the curve is described; while effecting the turns the body should be inclined as much as is practicable in maintaining a good balance.

In connection with our chapter on fast skating we give the records of speed attained by several of the fastest roller skaters known to the public at the present time, and in addition to this is presented a likeness of one who has, by defeating in nearly every contest the many skaters with whom he has been matched, well earned a title as the champion fast skater of America.

KENNETH A. SKINNER.

The illustration represents the subject of our sketch in racing costume.

Mr. Skinner commenced roller skating at Boston, Mass., in 1882, and in his first public race was defeated by Mr. F. G. Stumcke, to whom fifty feet start was given in this race, which occurred at the Olympian Rink in Boston.

In a race of two miles, at the same rink, for the championship of New England, May 20, 1883, Mr. Skinner defeated Messrs. O'Rourke and Alliston, and won in 8 min., 29¾ sec.

In another race of two miles Messrs. F. G. Stumcke and A. F. Rivard were defeated in 8 min., 4 sec.

In two races of two miles each, at the Olympian Rink, Newport, R. I., W. M. Drown, of Providence, R. I., was defeated.

At Nantasket Rink, Aug. 29, 1883, Mr. Skinner was defeated, in a one mile race, by Mr. Bert. C. Thayer, whom he afterward defeated at the same rink in a one mile race, Sept. 15, 1883. He again defeated Thayer, in 4 min., 15¾ sec., at the opening of the Institute Rink in Boston.

In November, 1883, Mr. Skinner skated one mile, in 3 min., 43 sec. in a race with Mr. J. W. Wilson on a bicycle, the latter winning by two seconds.

At the Instiute Rink, Boston, Dec. 8, 1883, he defeated Mr. B. L. Bailey in a race of five miles. Time 22 min., 29¾ sec.

At the same rink Dec. 25, 1883, he skated two races of one mile each against Mr. J. W. Wilson on a bicycle, the latter winning each race by 12 inches and 3 inches respectively. Time 3 m., 59 sec. and 4 m., 5 sec.

At the Star Rink in Haverhill, Mass., Jan. 22, 1884, in a race of twenty miles (23¾ laps to a mile), with Mr. Ladd of Haverhill for the championship of America, the following time was recorded.

Skinner—1 h., 35 m., 7 sec.

Ladd—1 h., 37 m., 28 sec.

At the Institute Rink at Boston, March 3d, 1884, in a race of five miles, seven laps to a mile, the following time was recorded: First mile, Nate E. Clark, 3 m., 47½ sec. K. A. Skinner, 3 m., 47¾ sec. On the second mile Skinner passed Clark and recorded 3 m., 52¼ sec. for that mile. Clark then withdrew.

In a second race of five miles at Haverhill, Mass., 23¾ laps to a mile, Skinner won in 21 m., 37 sec. Clark's time, 21 m., 47 sec.

At Lynn, Mass., March 6th, in a race of four miles, 20 laps to a mile, Skinner won in 17 m., 36 sec. Clark's time, 17 m., 41 sec.

At Institute Rink, Boston, March 7th, race of five miles, Skinner, 20 m., 9¼ sec. Clark 22 m., 16 sec.

At Haverhill, March 12th, race of five miles, Mr. Skinner was defeated by Mr. Cole in 20 m., 41 sec., the record being 20 m., 48 sec. for Mr. Skinner.

NATE E. CLARK.

This young skater of Corry, Penn., gives us a record of roller skating that shows the best long distance time yet made within our knowledge, and has also proved himself a formidable rival of the best short distance skaters. Mr. Clark writes us as follows :

" The first race I ever skated was against thirteen contestants, in Cleveland, Ohio, a half hour race for a gold medal, which I won. The distance accomplished, 5½ miles, was considered remarkable at that time. I have never heard of my 24 hour record being beaten."

Mr. Clark gives us the following record :

213 miles in 24 hours, at Dayton, Ohio.
100 " " 8 h., 27 m., " "
104 " " 10 hours " "
5 " " 19 m., 44 sec.
3 " " 12 m., 20 sec., at Cleveland, O.
2 " " 7 m., 56 sec., at Dayton, O.
15 " " 1 hour, at Cleveland, O.

W. C. TEGETHOFF.

This fast roller skater of Cleveland, Ohio, gives us the most remarkable record of time yet brought to our knowledge, having skated five miles in 18 m., 37 sec., and scoring one mile in 3 m., 15 sec., in the same race, which occurred at Cleveland, in a rink of 17½ laps to a mile.

In another race at Cleveland, Mr. Tegethoff skated three miles in 10 m., 24 sec., an average rate of 3 m., 28 sec. for a mile. Mr. W. H. Van Tine time-keeper, and Mr. Geo. Harrison (at that time manager of the rink) scorer of laps.

Both of these races occurred in February (16th and 26th) 1882, and we have not learned of any other such wonderful record having been made upon roller skates.

THE GAME OF POLO.

THE modern game of Polo on Skates is the game of Hockey (well-known to proficient ice-skaters), adapted to the limits of a skating rink. It is a game that can be made very attractive to spectators, as well as to the players, if skillfully played under proper rules and regulations. It should be a game to be won by skill in skating and tactics, and not by force. Games played without skill and by force alone, may please the few who enjoy roughness, but will not be tolerated by the more refined class of people visiting the rinks where a higher grade of entertainment is offered.

As the participant in and witness of skillfully played games of Hockey, we have learned by experience that such games excite an interest on the part of spectators, as is never developed toward the same game if played in a rough and tumble manner that likens it to a kicking and wrestling match. Our more recent observations of Polo convince us that the same elements will govern the success of this game, and in submitting the following rules we do so in the belief that their general adoption and observance will serve toward eliminating some of the roughness and developing greater skill in tactics and scientific methods. We have endeavored to present these rules and regulations in a manner that will enable new clubs without other assistance to properly lay out a Polo field and practice the game in accordance therewith. Only suggestions, and not rules for playing the game, would be of practical use. Each player and each team must play in accordance with the experience and skill in tactics acquired.

Players should constantly bear in mind that this is a game to be played with the ball on the ground or skating surface. Drive the ball and "shinny" it on the surface, instead of "batting" it into the air. The rules allow the goals to be three feet or not more than four feet high, as agreed upon by the contesting teams. We would recommend that three feet be the height adopted for goals.

Low play and a light ball are important features of this game, and should be adopted everywhere. Without due attention to this suggestion there is the liability of spectators incurring the risk of being hit by the ball. The occurrence of a child or lady thus receiving a blow in the face would do much toward driving Polo out of the rink.

Many suggestions might be offered in regard to match games; the teams could be drilled to perform skating movements around the rink with the precision of military companies, upon entrance to the skating surface, and at the finish come to the stations of "attention" (see Rule IX).

Although these rules may prove to be imperfect, we have tried to make them concise and plain to the understanding, wishing rather to omit some good features possible to be added hereafter, rather than risk introducing innovations liable to prove objectionable.

We have briefly offered a few of the many suggestions that could be made in regard to the means whereby the game of Polo on Skates may take a high rank as an athletic game of skill, and it is to further this object that we now submit these rules to the public. And as the best results may be attained by comparing and combining the experience of many, we ask polo players everywhere to aid in the improvement and promotion of the game by communicating their views to the

Publisher of the American Polo Rules,
P. O. box 1898, Portland, Me.

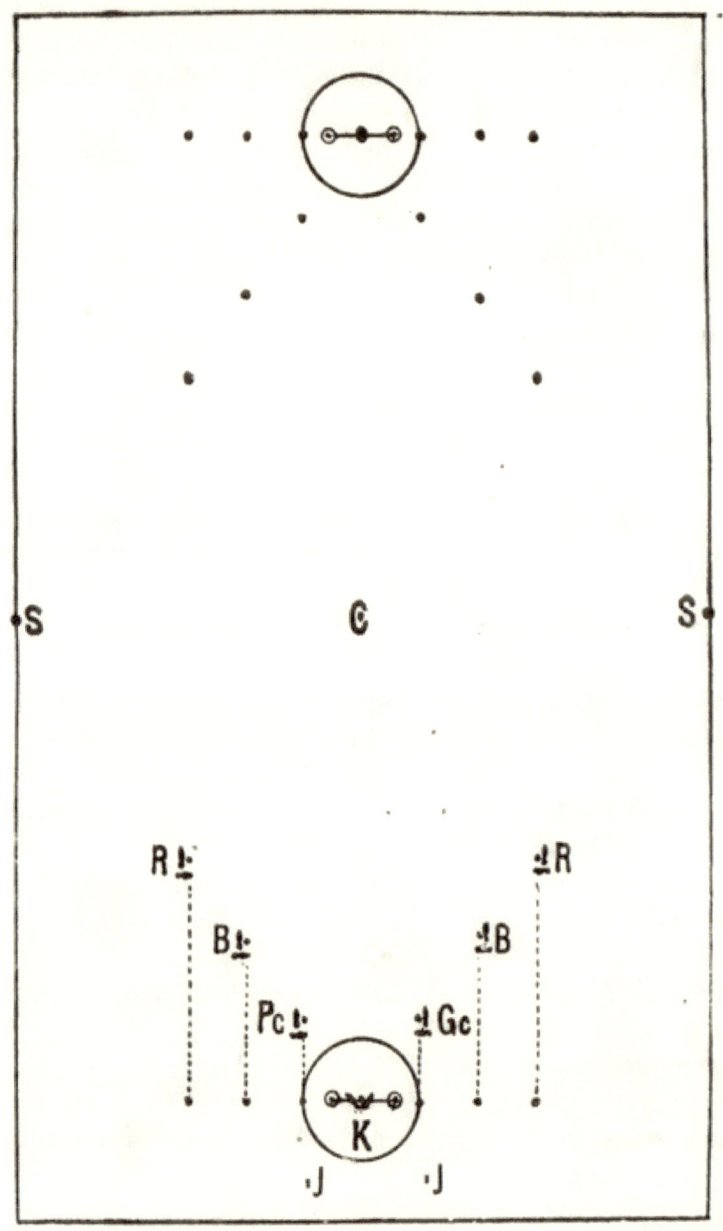

EXPLANATION OF DIAGRAM.

The illustration shows a field of rectangular form with a width three-fifths of its extreme length. Of course these bounds are not arbitrary, but are to be fixed in accordance with the proportions of the skating surface of any rink, and the relative positions of the players are always in proportion to the size and form of the field.

The exact location of each of the various stations and points defined, and indicated by the letters of reference, is shown by the dots.

K—The Goal-keeper's station or goal-center, upon each side of which are shown the positions of the *goal-posts*, with the *goal-line* drawn between them, and the whole inclosed within the *goal-circle*.

Pc—The Point-cover's station, on the Goal-keeper's left.

Gc—The Goal-cover's station, on the Goal-keeper's right.

B-B—The right and left Backers' stations

R-R—The right and left Rushers' stations.

S-S—The middle point of side boundaries.

C—The ball station, or middle point of a straight line between goal-centers.

J-J—The judges' stations, which are respectively behind the "attention" stations of the Goal-cover and Point-cover at the start of a game or innings, and at such distance back as will align each with a Rusher and the Goal-keeper.

The referee should stand at "S," upon either side, at the start.

The letters on the diagram indicate the players in the position of "ready."

The dotted lines indicate the movement from the position of "attention."

The players on the left of the goal are represented as

standing each with the left foot forward, and the players on the right each with the right foot forward.

This gives uniformity of appearance, and the same positions of the feet should be observed when at "attention."

The rules provide that at the signal "go," all four "rushers" shall move from their stations. How far each one moves depends upon the tactics of each player and the directions of his team captain. Ordinarily the right or left rusher of a team is instructed to rush for the ball, and the other to tarry so as to receive the ball if an opposing rusher first moves the ball.

The instant the ball is moved from its station of rest all the other players are released. Ordinarily the Point-cover is instructed by his captain to proceed at once and as quickly as possible to the station of the opposite Point-cover, where he is to play throughout each inning. Thus the opposing point-covers exchange places; so that during an inning each goal has its goal-cover, to aid the Goal-keeper and guard or cover his goal, and the opposing point-cover is in a similar position to guard or cover the play of his team.

When an inning is in progress, the rushers, backers and goal-keepers play according to their own judgment and the directions of their team captains. The judges remain in the rear of and near the goal. The referee follows the ball as much as is practical, his important duties requiring constant watchfulness.

The advantages of the field as shown are very apparent. The field can be quickly and easily marked out upon the surface, and it provides for a method and precision of move-ment (see Rule IX), in starting the game and innings, such as will aid spectators in comprehending the game, and effect a saving of time by enabling the judges and referee to see at a glance that the players are in proper position at the start.

After once accurately fixed, the goal-center, the stations of each rusher, and of the ball at rest, should be marked in a permanent manner by painting or otherwise upon the skating surface. The other stations, including those of the judges, may be readily located at any time by alignment with the Rushers' stations and the goal-center, if not permanently marked on the surface.

The stations assigned for the judges and referee are designed for the start merely. Under these regulations there is " a place for every man, and every man in his place " before the signal " go " is given to start the game. Uniformity in appearance of the field, and of each team of players, is thus attained, and in addition to this it may be seen that the stations are fixed by a system of practical utility.

When the players are at their stations in the position of " ready," the referee standing at "S" can at a glance see if the players of each team on that side are aligned in their proper places. As the station of each judge is on the continuation of the same line, the judges can see that all the players are in proper position on line, while in addition to this, the position of the referee enables him to see in line half the players of each team, as also to view the ball at the start. Thus each line of players is under the direct supervision of a judge, so that if any one moves forward from his station in the slightest degree before the proper time, it may be observed at once.

The judges should remain at their respective stations until all the players have been released by the starting of the ball. Thereafter the judges must remain near their allotted goals, and always in such a position as not to obstruct the players or the ball.

THE AMERICAN SKATERS' POLO RULES.

I. The Team.

1. Each team of players shall consist of seven persons, to be designated as follows; one Goal-keeper, two Rushers, two Backers, one Goal-cover, one Point-cover.

2. A substitute may be appointed in case of an injury to any player (see Rule XIII).

3. In championship matches no person shall play as a member of any team, who has played in a championship match within thirty days, as a member or player of another team, and all the contesting players must have been members of their respective teams for at least thirty days next previous to the match.

II. The Goals.

1. The goals shall each be formed by means of upright goal-posts, six feet apart, unless otherwise determined by the captains of the contesting teams; distance measured from center of posts, which shall be set not less than ten feet from the end bounds.

2. The goal-posts. shall be of a uniform height, of four feet or not less than three feet, and each of a diameter not exceeding two inches. The posts of each goal to be set on a line at right angles to the center line from goal to goal.

3. The distance between the goals, as also the bounds, should be fixed in accordance with the size of the rink where the game is played, and determined upon by the captains of the contesting teams.

4. The goal-line and the exact position of the posts shall be plainly marked upon the surface so as to indicate the goal bounds when the posts are displaced.

III. The Stick.

The stick shall not exceed one inch in diameter at any part, four feet in extreme length, nor one pound (16 ounces avoirdupois) weight.

The stick may be of any material, and any covering shall be measured as part of the stick.

IV. The Ball.

The ball shall be of three inches diameter, and not exceeding six ounces (avoirdupois) weight.

V. The Judges.

. 1. There shall be four judges; two appointed by the captain of each contesting team.

2. Two judges shall remain behind or near each goal during the progress of a game; the two judges for one goal to have been appointed each by the captain of the opposing team.

3. The duties of the judges shall be to decide upon the winning of goals and claims for fouls at their respective stations. In all cases of disagreement by the judges, final decision shall be given by the referee.

4. A time-keeper shall be appointed by the judges or a majority of them, and he shall be under the direction of the referee.

VI. The Referee.

1. There shall be one referee, who must be well informed in regard to the rules of the game, and appointed by the captains of the contesting teams. All decisions of the referee shall be final unless otherwise provided for by the rules or special agreement.

2. The duties of the referee shall be to decide upon all questions submitted to him by the judges, or upon such questions as do not come before the judges, that are submitted to him by the captains of the contesting teams.

3. It shall be the referee's duty to start the game; to stop it at the end of an inning, or upon failure of compliance with the rules by either team, as hereinafter provided; and at the request of the team captains he may declare "drawn," or "off," any inning.

4. It shall be the duty of the referee to keep a correct score and record of each game as it is played.

5. The referee may stop the game at any time for a violation of the rules, or for any extraordinary occurrence not provided for by the rules that may in his judgment demand it.

VII. The Game.

1. The game shall consist of three or five "goals." as may be determined before the contest by the captains of the teams, the team adjudged the winner of two goals or three goals respectively, the same being a majority, shall be the winner of the game.

2. A goal shall be won when the ball is fairly driven from the direction of the opposite goal, through the goal below the top of the goal-posts, and entirely beyond a line drawn

across the goal from center to center of its posts, and known
as the "goal-line." Or if the ball is thus driven over the.
goal-line, within the bounds named, the goal is won.

3.   The time for a game shall be limited to forty-five minutes unless otherwise agreed upon. If the stipulated time
expires before a majority of goals is won by either team, a
five-goal game may be awarded to the team that has won
two goals out of three, such award to be made by a plurali-
ty vote of the judges and referee. In other cases games
not won within the stipulated time may be declared
" drawn," by the referee.

VIII.   Stations of Players.

The stations of the players at the start shall be plainly
marked upon the skating surface. When in the position of
"ready" prepared to receive the signal "go," the players
shall be stationed as follows:

1.   The *Goal-keeper's* station is at the goal-center.

2.   The stations of the *Goal-cover* and *Point-cover* are
each side and in advance of the goal, one-third the distance
from the goal-center to the Rusher's station, and on line between the Rusher and goal-center, the Goal-cover's station
being on the Goal-keeper's right, and the Point-cover's station on his left.

3.   The two *Backers'* stations are each on the line between
the Rusher and the goal-center, and two-thirds the distance
from the goal-center to the Rushers' station.

4.   The two *Rushers'* stations are each at a point half way.
from the goal-center to the middle point of the side boundary, at the center of a line drawn between these two points.

The referee shall decide by lot the first position of each
team. Each team contesting shall guard its respective goal
throughout each inning of a game, and at the end of every
inning the teams shall exchange places.

IX.   The Signals.

The signals for summoning the players to the field, and
starting and stopping the game, shall be given by the referee, and unless otherwise determined by the captains of the
contesting teams, shall be as follows:

1.   *Attention.* This is the first signal, given by one long
prolonged whistle, and at its summons each team shall take
its respective place, the players to be in line each side of the
goal, in proper order of places; the Goal-keeper on the goal-
line, the Goal-cover and Point-cover at the right and left,
outside the goal-posts, the right and left Backers next on

line, and the right and left Rushers at each end of the line.
The players of the opposing team to be in similar line at
the other goal.

When thus in the position of "attention," the players of
a team should be such a distance apart as will place them
directly in the rear of their respective stations, to which
they will advance in parallel lines at the summons of the
next signal.

2. *Ready.* This signal is given by two short whistles, and
when sounded, the players of both teams shall advance to
their respective stations, thus changing the straight front
line to the form of the letter V. When thus in position, the
referee shall call aloud the word "ready," and the captain
of each team shall respond by repeating the word "ready"
to the referee, who, immediately thereafter, shall start the
playing by giving the next signal.

3. *Go.* One short whistle given by the referee shall be
the signal "go," to start an inning, and it shall mean "stop,"
when given during the progress of a game. At the signal
"go," the Rushers leave their stations by "rushing" toward the ball, and the game begins.

The close of each inning shall be announced by the signal "attention," upon which all the players shall at once re-
sume the positions first taken under this signal, prepared
to respond to the following signal "ready" for the next
innings.

X. THE START.

1. All games and innings shall be started by the referee.
After the teams have been called to the field and are in the
position of attention, the referee shall place the ball at its
station of rest, at the middle point of a straight line from
goal-center to opposite goal-center.

2. When the referee gives the signal "go" (see Rule IX.,
sec. 3), all the "Rushers" shall move from their stations,
and any one or all of them may "rush" for the ball.

3. No other player shall leave his station until the ball is
moved from its place of rest, when every player becomes
free to act as he pleases under the rules.

XI. BOUNDS.

1. The field bounds shall be the skating surface of the
rink, unless otherwise agreed upon.

2. When the ball goes out of bounds during the progress
of an inning, and rebounds to the skating surface again, the
game shall proceed without interruption.

3. When the ball goes out of bounds and does not immediately return, the game shall be suspended, and the referee, with least possible delay, shall place the ball four feet within the boundary line at the point where the ball went out, and the game shall be resumed at the signal of the word "go" given by the referee.

4. And the referee may thus temporarily suspend the game on account of the "ball out of bounds," whenever the ball is returned in such a manner as shall, in the judgment of the referee, demand such suspension.

5. There shall be a circle plainly marked upon the surface around the goal, and known as the goal-circle, to be of five feet radius from the goal-center.

After the game is begun, and during the progress of an inning no player except the goal-keeper shall stop within the goal-circle, under penalty of a foul, except when the ball passes within this circle.

No person shall be allowed within the field boundaries during the progress of a game, except the contesting players, the judges, and the referee.

XII.   CLAIMS FOR FOULS.

1. A claim of "foul" may be made by any of the players of the contesting teams during the progress of a game, by calling to the referee the word "foul," and some word or words to indicate the nature of the foul claimed, as "foul blow," "foul kick," etc.

2. If the claim of "foul" is not at once allowed by the referee, or the "stop" signal given, the game shall proceed without interruption. If the claim is allowed, the referee announces the fact by sounding the signal (one short whistle), to stop the game. The referee may also stop the game whenever in doubt about a claim for foul.

3. After the game is stopped for a claim of foul, it shall be started by the referee placing the ball as near as possible where the foul occurred, and giving the signal "go."

XIII.   DEFINITION OF FOULS.

It shall be deemed a foul:

1. If any player intentionally strikes, kicks, or trips another player during the progress of a game.

2. If any player catches, strikes, or stops the ball with his hand, or drives the ball by kicking,—but any player may use his feet for stopping the ball, and the *Goal-keeper* may stop or drive the ball with his feet.

3. Any player using skates with the rollers covered or

smeared with any substance not a part of the construction of the skates, or such as may be injurious to the skating surface, shall be declared guilty of a foul, and prohibited taking any further part in the game in progress.

XIV. PENALTIES FOR FOULS.

Two fouls within the goal-circle adjudged against one team during the progress of an inning may be declared as a goal for the opposing team.

Three fouls anywhere, adjudged against one team during the progress of an inning, shall be declared as a goal for the opposing team.

XV. ACCIDENTS.

1. If a player is disabled during the progress of a game, by personal injury, illness, breakage or loss of a skate, or otherwise, the referee shall stop the game, upon request of the captain of either team, and after permitting a delay not exceeding three minutes, shall call the teams to the position of "ready," and start the game again.

2. If any player is disabled so as to prevent his continuing the game, a substitute may be appointed by the captain of the team thus deprived of a member, and as much delay for such purpose shall be allowed as is deemed necessary by the referee.

THESE RULES HAVE BEEN ADOPTED BY THE MAINE POLO LEAGUE.

NOTE.

In all games played under these rules the decisions of the referee are final.

There can be no exceptions to the rules unless previously stipulated in the terms for match games. It may be desirable to use a ball not fully corresponding to Rule IV, and any such exception or change can be effected by special stipulation or agreement as above indicated.

RULE XIII.

SECTION 4. If a player drives the ball, or intentionally stops it, while any part of his person touches the surface, he shall be declared guilty of a foul.

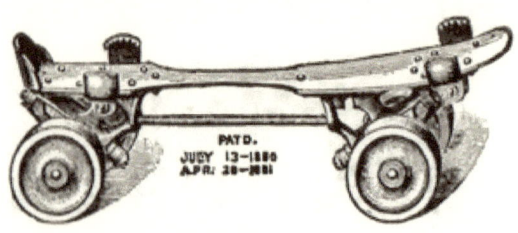

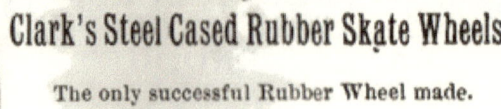

ꙮOLD꙳ORCHARDꙮ

꙳SKATING꙳RINKꙮ

OLD ORCHARD BEACH, MAINE.

C. B. WHITNEY, - Manager.

One of the largest and finest summer rinks in America, being nearly 200 feet in length and 100 feet wide, with a skating surface of nearly 11,000 square feet, built of the finest kiln-dried yellow birch, and has the reputation of being the finest skating surface in the United States.

It has accommodations for 2000 spectators, while nearly 1000 persons can skate at one time.

It is lighted by electric lights and gas.

The interior of the rink is made especially attractive by a brilliant series of decorations, designed expressly for this rink.

MUSIC has received special attention, being furnished by a carefully selected Band and Orchestra of first class musicians.

All the appointments are as nigh perfect as can be, and the highest character of rink management will be maintained.

꙳S꙳E꙳S꙳S꙳I꙳O꙳N꙳S꙳

MORNING, FROM 10 TO 12.
AFTERNOON, FROM 2.30 TO 5.
EVENING, FROM 7.30 TO 10.15.

MUSIC AT EACH SESSION.

ATTRACTIONS, of which due notice will be given, will be of the very highest order. Nothing but first class talent has been secured.

This Rink has one of the strongest Polo Clubs in New England.

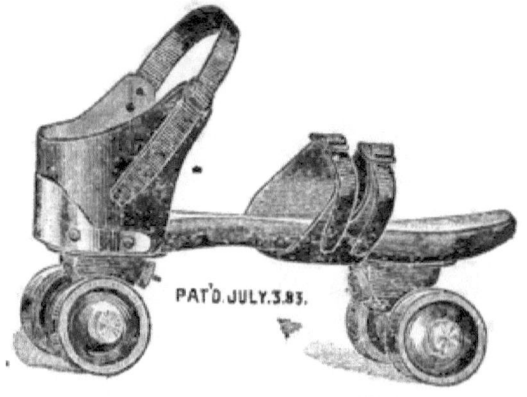

WILL BE READY FOR BUSINESS.

SEASON OF 1884.

THE

MT. DESERT BRANCH

OF THE

Maine Central Railroad,

GIVING

THREE DAILY TRAINS

BETWEEN

BANGOR

AND

BAR HARBOR,

Connecting with through trains from and to

BOSTON, PORTLAND, AND ST. JOHN.

Express Trains, Boston and Bar Harbor, in 10 1-2 hours.

BREAKFAST AT BOSTON. {ENTIRE TRIP BY DAYLIGHT} **SUPPER AT BAR HARBOR.**

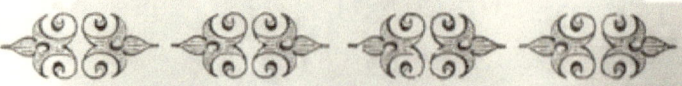

www.ingramcontent.com/pod-product-compliance
Lightning Source LLC
Chambersburg PA
CBHW032156010726
47493CB00008BA/2719